Pull Me Closer

Lauren H. Kelley

LOVESPIN PUBLISHING | ATLANTA

LoveSpin

LOVESPIN PUBLISHING | ATLANTA

This is an original publication of LoveSpin Publishing, LLC.

Published by LoveSpin Publishing
ISBN 978-0-9898714-2-6

Cover design by LoveSpin Publishing.

Contents

Acknowledgments

To my fabulous editor Yolanda Barber who challenged me every step of the way. To my husband, friends and extended family members who encouraged me to pursue my dream. Thank you all.

PULL ME CLOSER

First in A Series | A Suits in Pursuit Novel

Lauren H. Kelley

LoveSpin

LOVESPIN PUBLISHING | ATLANTA

CHAPTER ONE

Sunday, June 25, 2011

"I won't compromise. If that means I have to be alone, that's what I'll do." Kerrigan lifted her bare left hand, staring at the finger where the wedding band rested on normal women her age. "Don't take this the wrong way, Ash, but that's the difference between you and me. I'm looking for Mr. Right, and you're looking for Mr. Right in the Moment."

Ashley laughed hoarsely. "Correction, I'm looking for Mr. Perfectly Fine to Fu..."

Kerrigan choked a laugh back, interrupting her. "Ash! Don't be crude."

"You know me. I speak the truth, even when the truth is ugly."

Kerrigan loved her best friend, but she often thought Ashley could benefit from a filter. "I like truth, but must you be so primitive?"

"I have needs, and you do too if you'd stop thinking with your head long enough to feel the yearning between your thighs. You're looking for Mr. Perfect and newsflash, he doesn't exist."

Ashley quipped, the words rolling off her tongue with the slightest hint of bitterness.

"I'm not looking for anyone." Kerrigan paused, thrumming her index finger on her temple. "I'm watching that motivational speaker Laura Stephens." Shuffling over to the sofa, she plopped down, narrowed her eyes and mouthed silent words, mimicking the talk show host who must have consumed one too many energy drinks. "Laura says that if I want to make my life sing, then I simply need to take the first step." Kerrigan muttered into the phone, her tone mocking. "She's right about one thing—I have to try something new. I've lived in Texas, Chicago, Los Angeles and New York in less than five years." Her chest tightened, and she wiped light beads of moisture that dampened her forehead. "God! Just saying that stresses me out. I can't do this anymore."

"Kerri, you've been a road warrior for eight years. No one can keep that pace forever. Send me your résumé. I'm biased, but living together in the same city will be so exciting."

Stretching her legs across the sage microfiber sofa, Kerrigan grabbed her laptop from the cocktail table and huffed. "All right, fine. I'll email my resume to you now." She hadn't meant to sound annoyed. "Sorry, Ash, I know you're only looking out for me. The thought of moving to another new city is slightly terrifying. You know, if I could open my own little boutique and settle into a quiet non-turbulent existence, I would."

"Kerri, you know I love you, but you've talked about that boutique for years, and you haven't done anything to move that dream forward. Besides, marketing is your thing—you're a genius. Moving to Atlanta might be the best move for you. There's so much to do, and so many people to meet. Even you might find somebody special."

Kerrigan rolled her eyes and signed into her email account. "What's that supposed to mean? I've done my fair share of dating, thank you very much. Sure, I haven't dated tons of men like you have, but I don't have the time, energy or patience, and I have high standards."

"Uh huh. Standards? Seriously Kerri, when was the last time you had a serious relationship or short-term boy-toy for that matter? When's the last time you went on a date?" Ashley's sarcasm made Kerrigan cringe.

"Ash, I seriously think something is wrong with me. I swear I'm a loser magnet. If there's a loser within a thirty-mile radius of me, that moron will sniff-me out." Kerrigan rubbed the throbbing vein in her neck. "That's why I haven't dated in almost three years."

"God! Three years, Kerri? I didn't realize how much time had passed. I wouldn't survive," Ashley scoffed.

She threw her head back and groaned. "Do you remember when I dated Michael the finance guy for two weeks?"

"Yeah, whatever happened to him?" Ashley asked, the tone of her voice rising.

Kerrigan huffed, and then uploaded her resume to the blank email message. "I thought he'd bore me to death. He spoke three sentences the entire two weeks we dated. Remember the dude with all the tattoos?"

"He wasn't even your type. You saw his body and went berserk," Ashley chided.

Kerrigan couldn't debate the truth. She did like the way his biceps bulged. "I can't believe he walked five miles from the bus stop to my house for our first date. The whole time, he kept trying to put his grimy little hands all over me." The thought made Kerrigan's stomach flip-flop. "He repulsed me. Did I tell you that he asked me for bus fare to get home?" Laughing so hard, Ashley erupted into a snort. Kerrigan clutched her side, soothing the ache from the laugh she so desperately needed. She ran the back of her index finger under each eye, wiping tears away.

"Like the date from hell with tattoo boy hadn't been enough, Craig holds the 'ultimate loser award'." Kerrigan dug her nails into the sofa's seat cushion. Just the memory of his beady eyes made her want to yell at the top of her lungs. "He told a friend of his that I wasn't good enough for his family, and I was only smart enough to open my legs for him." Releasing a long sigh, she sank into the sofa and pushed her bottom lip out into a pout.

Ashley groaned. "Okay, so you've gone out with a few duds. Who hasn't?"

"I'm traumatized. Most men just don't excite me. If there's no chemistry, sizzle or magic, then why should I bother, right?" Kerrigan chewed on her bottom lip.

"Hell, what if the chemistry comes later? You'd never get the chance to find out if you swear off all men."

"You remember my theory about men," she said, sure that Ashley must be rolling her eyes by this time. "I'm not swearing off all men. I'm just avoiding most of them. If a man wants me, he'll have to do some serious chasing, there has to be chemistry and well … he has to meet my criteria."

"Yeah, I know all about your theory on the four general types of men." The acid in Ashley's tone made Kerrigan laugh.

She covered her heart with her hand, a pseudo gesture of being touched. "Ash, I can't believe you remember my misters—Mr. Self-absorbed, Mr. Obsessive, Mr. Nonchalant and Mr. Chivalrous."

"How can I forget? Mr. Self-absorbed is the overly confident, arrogant bastard who I always seem to attract. Definitely stay away from his type. I dated Mr. Obsessive. He was so insecure and smothered me to the point that I almost suffocated."

"Who? Too-tall Paul?"

"Yes! Thought I'd lose my damn mind. His lanky ass was always there, everywhere." Ashley quipped.

Kerrigan laughed. Paul wasn't so bad, but being paired with Ashley, the ultimate independent woman, had been a mistake. "Well, when I did date I'd always end up with Mr. Nonchalant. I like a laid-back guy, but there comes a time when a man has to do something with his life. Besides, living in a cardboard box is overrated. Now Mr. Chivalrous …"

Ashley interrupted. "I hate to be the bearer of bad news, but you and every woman hoping for her proverbial knight in freaking shining armor wants Mr. Chivalrous," Ashley chided. "Kerri, I know you believe in your theory about men, but I think you use this as an excuse to push men away. You're gorgeous, intelligent, fun and charming. If you get this job, I'm going to hook you up."

Taking the throw from the sofa's arm, Kerrigan wrapped it around her shoulders and nestled into her usual spot for moping. "Ash, I'm not looking for perfection. I want a man who's confident, but not arrogant, who's not afraid to show affection, but won't smother me, and who simply enjoys life, but has goals, dreams, hopes—a job."

"Uh huh," Ashley said, and then released an exaggerated sigh.

"I want a man who's considerate and caring—someone who respects me."

"You may as well include something about his looks," Ashley said, a snicker tickling her vocal chords.

Kerrigan nodded her head. "A good-looking man is a bonus. I'd settle for any man who has a pulse as long as he meets my criteria."

"And you think this man will ride into your life on his magical unicorn or appear on your doorstep wrapped up in a bow?

You have to put yourself out there, maybe even date if you want to find your man."

"I refuse to go out with a bunch of losers trying to find the right one. I want a man that leaves me breathless and makes me come alive." The thought of a man like this made Kerrigan's insides tingle.

"What you want is to fall in love," Ashley said, her tone soft.

Shifting her position on the sofa, Kerrigan glanced at the television. Muted, Laura Stephens flitted back and forth across the screen in a blur of colors making wild arm gestures, rambling on in silence. "I guess you're right. I do want to fall in love. I want to be wooed, and I won't settle for less."

"Wooed? Really?" Ashley laughed. "What you're looking for is a damn time machine, and I can't help you with that, but I can help you land a new job. I've got more info on those two jobs I told you about." Ashley's excitement seeped through the phone.

"Oh, that's great, Ash. Give me details on the positions."

"One is a junior account rep, and the other is a senior account rep position on our national accounts team."

Kerrigan frowned. A vision of her future flashed through her mind as she imagined herself sitting alone in an empty airport. "Ugh! That sounds like travel, and travel is exactly what I'm trying to avoid." Every Monday, schlepping to Los Angeles on the redeye, and then back to New York that evening by seven. Tomorrows hectic work schedule gave Kerrigan palpitations. She refused to think about the Wednesday meetings in Chicago.

"Well, I do know these positions are for local accounts. The clients are national players, but they're headquartered here in town. Very little travel required. The agency is small, has a laid-back environment and is located in the heart of downtown. The CEO is awesome."

Kerrigan's interest piqued. A fresh start in a new city is what she needed to help her regain control of the crazy that had become her life.

"I'll send your résumé to the hiring manager in the morning. Her name is Marie Henderson. Your background and experience is perfect. Leave the job to me. All you need to do now is find a place to live." She paused. "And Kerri, if you really want to find a man, maybe you need to open yourself to new experiences."

Kerrigan hit the send button on her email. "I'm going to try being more open-minded and open myself to new adventures, but I'm not compromising. I want my Mr. Right." Every night she sent a silent prayer heavenward. Kerrigan waited for this man, and he would be worth the wait.

***

A blaring sound jarred her from a deep sleep. Where am I? Who's calling this early? Kerrigan stretched across the hotel bed to the mahogany nightstand, her fingers almost unable to reach her iPhone. She hated overnight business trips and stays in a strange hotel room.

"Hello," she said, her thoughts muddled and not awake fully.

"Hi, may I speak with Kerrigan Mulls please?"

Staving off a yawn, "This is Kerrigan," she muttered.

"Hi, Kerrigan, this is Joan Washington, a recruiter with A.C. Advertising. I received your résumé. You have quite an impressive background. I'd like to bring you in to interview with Marie Henderson. Are you still interested in the junior account rep position?"

The woman's voice sounded too cheery for a five o'clock morning call. Kerrigan's foggy brain clearing a little, she remembered the time difference between Los Angeles and Atlanta.

She cleared her throat. "Yes, that's right." The words rolled off Kerrigan's tongue. She was impressed with the evidence of her grogginess expertly masked.

"Wonderful. I'll coordinate the schedule and be in touch later this week with details. If you pass the first round of interviews, expect to come back to meet with our CEO."

"Sounds fantastic, Joan. Thank you." She yawned, quickly muting the call.

She took her first step into the bathroom and looked at her haggard appearance. Tired, swollen eyes stared back. Her long wavy-curly mane needed some care and attention. She had the credentials and experience, but if she expected to land a new job and create the life she wanted, she needed to look the part. In desperate need of a makeover, Kerrigan made a hair appointment, treated herself to a manicure and pedicure, and planned a small shopping spree for her interview. She would be ready, and she would look damn good too.

***

Tuesday, July 12, 2011

"Sir, Kerrigan Mulls is here. Are you ready for her?" Brenda asked.

Axel frowned, but kept his attention turned to his computer. "Should I be ready for her? Who is she?" he barked.

Brenda's eyebrows pressed together and the toe of her square-tipped shoe tapped against the hardwood floor. "Kerrigan Mulls. She's interviewing for the junior account rep position in Marie's department. She's your eleven o'clock."

Grateful for an organized executive assistant like Brenda, "You know, I couldn't run this company without you," he said, gave her a quick glance and returned to his work.

Brenda's gaze settled on his humbled smirk. "I hope you remember that."

Axel Christensen was many things. Young. Hot. Successful. He didn't have a lot of patience. He wasn't particularly in the mood to conduct an interview today. His sexy little lunch date would be meeting him soon, and he couldn't wait to see Misty Scott again. Their conversation would be dull, and they had nothing in common, but then again, her brain didn't interest him.

Insisting that he meet every job candidate for the account rep positions, he cursed himself. The interviews were important, but he would make this one brief. Having become an excellent judge of character, he would know within minutes if Kerrigan Mulls would be the right person for the job.

Axel glanced at Brenda, whose arms were crossed, clutching a stack of papers against her chest. "All right, send her in," he relinquished his frown and turned back to the spreadsheet on his computer screen.

"Very good. I'll bring her in now." Brenda headed for the executive suite reception area where Kerrigan Mulls waited.

***

Kerrigan took in the contemporary, but elegant and expensive décor of the executive suite. The receptionists' counter where Brenda sat was sleek, and modern made of what looked like frosted glass over silver metal with the agency's name etched across the front. Lounge-style seats in navy leather sat in the lobby, and abstract prints in vivid hues hung around the room against stark white walls.

While waiting, Kerrigan pulled out a sheet of paper and read over her notes. She hadn't been able to find much information on A.C. Advertising or the CEO in her research, but she pegged him as a weasel, a fast-talking pitchman, despite Ashley's praise. Based on what she learned, he had been driven to succeed and had done quite well, having built the multi-million dollar advertising agency from the ground up. The position she wanted would support the company's growth and expansion plans by securing new business and additional revenue.

The heavy oak doors opened slowly and Brenda emerged, bustling over to her with a stack of paper and a file folder in hand. "Miss Mulls, Mr. Christensen will see you now. Do you need anything? Would you like a beverage, maybe some coffee?"

She eyed the woman with pity. She looked bogged down with all those items in her hands. "No, thank you—I'm fine. Please call me Kerrigan."

Standing, Kerrigan's hand ran down her skirt to smooth out the creases that had formed while she sat, and then she shook her hair into place. She leaned down, picked up her laptop bag, and followed Brenda through the set of oversized oak double doors that led into the CEO's office. Eyes darting throughout the space, she noted the décor, handsome like the man who sat behind the immaculately organized desk at the other end of the room.

The large office housed three meetings areas including a conference table to the right of the entrance flanked by a set of tall black bookcases. Her eyes landed on a long red leather sofa anchored against the wall near the large black desk where the CEO sat. She and Brenda approached two guest chairs in front of his desk, his eyes still riveted to his computer screen.

Brenda clutched her papers and folder tightly. "Mr. Christensen, this is Kerrigan Mulls. Kerrigan, this is our President and Chief Executive Officer, Axel Christensen." Brenda gave a half smile, and then walked briskly toward the massive doors, slipped passed the two of them leaving Kerrigan alone with him.

He didn't make the halfhearted effort to recognize her. Kerrigan stood there with her hands trembling and knees knocking, marveling at the young CEO. She didn't imagine the head of the company would be, well … so damn good-looking. Ashley omitting this information surprised her. Despite his appearance, she couldn't believe that her friend raved about working for the man. He seemed cold and distant. A far cry from awesome, as Ashley described him.

Though he wore an expensive, custom tailored suit, she could see the hard, chiseled man beneath. Axel Christensen was insanely and menacingly hot. A face sculpted to perfection, the man was a masculine work of art in living flesh.

His hand slid away from the mouse, he turned in her direction and lifted his eyes from the monitor. As soon as he stood, she warmed in an instant. Interviews always made Kerrigan nervous, or maybe the man glaring down at her caused her heart rate to increase and her breath to catch in her throat. The towering giant extended a mammoth hand to greet her in standard professional fashion. Placing her small jittery hand in his palm, her gaze crawled up his roughly six feet, five-inch frame to blazing blue eyes, a vivid complement to his tanned olive complexion and dark hair.

His brow pressed together forming a thick dark line across his creased forehead. Slowly relaxing the contorted muscles of his face, his puzzled expression melted away. "Hello." The sound of his deep silky voice stroked her ears, reverberating through her core in quakes. As he greeted her, she flustered at the overpowering intensity of his stark presence, athletic physique and raw sexual intonation of his simple one-word greeting.

She blinked. "Hi," she stammered back, unable to think of anything more intelligent to say. She hated interviews, and the CEO's good looks didn't help calm her nerves.

The searing heat of his imposing gaze landed on her flesh. His computer was no longer the most fascinating thing in the room. The lustful gaze of his eyes raking up and down her body left her exposed. Averting his glare, she fixed her sights on an unfastened button on his shirt. He seemed paralyzed, as though his brain held his next words prisoner. His laser focus continued scanning her over.

After the longest minute in her life passed, his eyes found hers again, and she held his stare. The intensity almost too much for her to bear, her knees were going to buckle and she would end up sprawled out on the hardwood floor—not a great way to make a first impression. How could one first time encounter with a man make her feel this way?

***

Mesmerized. Axel surrounded himself by beautiful women, but something about Kerrigan Mulls captivated him the minute his eyes landed on her. Taking in her beauty, he studied her delicate features and noticed the way her long dark hair cascaded down her back, tumbling over one shoulder in soft curls. Big, beautiful, hazel eyes looked up at him. He wanted to touch her flawless, caramel-coated skin and her plum-colored lips begged to be licked. The white blouse she wore gave him a tantalizing view of the cleavage that belonged to perky, round breasts. She wore a fitted gray skirt that hugged her small curvaceous frame. Long slender, shapely legs extended from beneath the hem of her skirt, leading down to feet adorned by a pair of stylish silver-toned peep-toe stilettos. She had to be the most beautiful woman his eyes ever probed.

Her hand trembling in his, he clutched her fingers tightly to steady her tremors. An electrifying current surged through him, and the background of his surrounding office faded away. He wondered if she felt the spark too. The quiet gasp that escaped her lips told him that she did. He watched her slender, bronze fingers slide out of his grasp as she withdrew her hand from his. Rubbing her left palm, she caressed the tangible impression he left on her.

Her eyes grew large, startled by the sound of him clearing his throat. “Please take a seat Miss, Mrs. Mulls,” he said.

A nervous smile stretched across her face like rays of sunlight stretched across the horizon. Losing her balance, she stumbled, gripped the edge of his desk and then landed roughly in the leather guest chair behind her. “I, I’m … Miss Mulls. Just call me Kerrigan,” she stammered as a hint of color marked her cheeks.

Confining his bemused smirk, he covered his mouth with his hand and rubbed his chin. He sat and his pants tightened around his growing erection, making him uncomfortable. Axel had never become aroused at a first introduction. He leaned back in his chair, rested his right foot on the opposite knee, and gave his groin reprieve. His hands folded, he placed them on the back of his neck with his bent arms spanned out. Perhaps his casual posture would help her relax.

“Well Kerrigan, tell me about your background.”

Her eyes traced his distended muscles through the long sleeves of his white shirt. “Well…” She shifted in her seat crossing her left leg over the right, uncrossing them, and then crossing them again, right over left. Finally, she stilled. “I’ve been in the advertising business for seven years. I’m good at what I do. My clients trust me to come up with creative strategies to expand their market share and grow revenue.”

He changed positions to improve his view, his elbows resting on the desk now. "Can you tell me about your latest campaign success?"

She looked away for several moments, as though pondering his question. "I developed the marketing strategy to support the expansion of Tip Toe Shoes over six national markets with an exciting new campaign targeted to women ages eighteen to forty. Our creative team went to work, and the radio spots and television commercials proved successful. They're entering the Atlanta and Chicago markets this year." Her voice trembled slightly when she spoke, and he wondered if she had interview anxiety or if her nervous energy resulted from something else, perhaps him.

Continuing his appraisal, his eyes slid down her naked legs. "That's interesting. How do you earn your clients' trust?" he asked.

"Like any relationship, it takes equal partnership and commitment to build trust. I learn everything I can about their business, understand their audience and find out what they need, want and expect, and then I deliver. I want them feeling satisfied with the experience and results. They'll come back for more."

Smart. He liked that. "How much new revenue did the client bring in after the campaign launched?" He watched as the answer touched her eyes, and then words formed on her lips like fresh morning dew on a leaf.

"Three months after the campaign launched, their revenues doubled. What you really want to know is how much the agency profited, right?"

Bringing his hand to his chin, he stroked the base of the smile that she coaxed. He liked her a lot. "I do."

"The account brings in about two million dollars a year for three years, incremental revenue for the agency."

She pulled out her laptop to show samples of her work.

He stood and walked from behind his desk. "I can see your work better this way." Taking a seat next to her, he pulled the chair closer to her, enjoying her closeness and sweet floral scent that teased his nostrils. "Let's see what you've got, Miss Mulls."

Although a little tense, he marveled at Kerrigan's professionalism and the ease with which she conducted herself. He knew he could be an intense man.

Her lips curved upward into a smile. *Beautiful.*

"You may not like the creative execution and neither did my boss at the time, but he trusted me to make the call, and I didn't back off. I knew the client and audience well, and I had confidence that my strategy would get results," she said.

He intimidated some of the most seasoned account reps who worked for him. They refused to challenge him, offer a rebuttal or share an original thought, and they cowered in his presence. She had the gusto to stand up for what she believed right. *Tenacity.* He admired her confidence.

Adjusting her laptop so he could get a better view of the ads, his arm brushed against hers. *Soft.* "I don't want you to have any misgivings about this position. Tell me why you want to leave your current job. Why do you want to work for me?"

Interested in her in many more ways than one, he was confident that he could lure her into a date, but he wanted to know if she could handle the junior-level job.

She wiggled in her seat again. "Well, I'm relocating to the city, and your agency has an outstanding reputation. I think my experience will be a complement to your team. Personally, I need a change and a new start. I've traveled my entire career. I want stability, and frankly I'm ready for the next chapter in my life to begin."

He studied her in silence, and then slowly, methodically flashed his deadliest smile. "Change is good. I hope your next chapter brings you everything you want."

"Me too," she said, her timid gaze reaching his leer.

"Do you have any questions for me?"

"Yes, one. What are you looking for?"

He raised his brow, and then regurgitated her earlier words, surprised by her question. "Someone who can give me what I need and want, and make me come back for more," he said, deepening his voice to a baritone pitch and watching her response.

Kerrigan nodded. "I think I can do that," she said straight-faced without the slightest hint of tease, either having missed or choosing to ignore the duality of his answer. She possessed an innocent quality that he found alluring.

"I'm counting on you to," he said.

He studied her face again, sure that his heavy gaze made her uncomfortable, but he couldn't keep his eyes away. *Intelligent. Beautiful.* Blood rushed to his groin and his pulse raced. With his temperature rising, he tugged at the constrictive collar around his neck.

Her eyes followed his hands as he unfastened the second button on his shirt. "You're talented. Since you're sitting in my office, obviously you're the leading candidate. Marie is ready to make an offer." *I'm ready to make a different offer altogether.* "What are your salary requirements?"

"I'm willing to negotiate. Last year, I made one hundred and thirty thousand dollars. I expect at least that."

In a move rare for a shrewd executive like himself, he felt the need to protect her, to take care of her. "Kerrigan, you took the bait. In a negotiation, never throw out the figure first. If I didn't have the best intentions, I could easily take advantage of you." Her courage to create the new life she wanted fueled his admiration.

"What would you say if I offered you a salary of one hundred and seventy thousand dollars, plus commission?"

Her eyebrows shot up. She didn't say anything immediately, thinking over his offer. "I would say yes; however, I have one stipulation."

He stiffened, clenched his jaw tight and narrowed his icy gaze on her. His offer had been more than generous. She was going to find out her mistake if she thought he would negotiate. *Just like all the rest.* "And what is your stipulation, Miss Mulls?"

"I don't need a salary that large. I'd like my commission to be deducted from my paycheck and donated to a charity of your choosing."

His eyes stretched wide, and the tense muscles in his face softened. He never liked to be wrong, but this time had been the exception. *Kind.* "That's an unusual, but considerate counter. We've got a deal." Getting a glimpse of her character more than intrigued him. No woman had ever turned down his money, let alone encouraged him to donate to a charitable organization.

Light danced in her eyes as the ends of her lips curled upward. "Great! When do I start?" Enthusiasm lit up her entire face, making her eyes sparkle.

He melted. A woman who was as stunning inside as her outside was a novelty to him.

He leaned in closer, watching her big round eyes and surveying her movements. "Good. Take a week to settle in, and then start the following Monday. How does that sound?"

Kerrigan planted her eyes on her laptop. "That sounds great. I'll have time to find an apartment and get unpacked."

A knock at the door interrupted their conversation. Whipping around in his chair, he scowled as he watched Brenda tramp in and intrude uninvited.

"Mr. Christensen. Misty Scott is holding on the line for you." Clamping his teeth, he balled his fists. "She's calling about your meeting today. Shall I put her through?" Brenda asked, her voice irritated.

Glad that Brenda hadn't referred to his meeting as a date, his hands loosened. "Please cancel my meeting with um, Miss Scott. I'll follow-up with her later." Brenda nodded, and with heavy steps clobbering the floor, she slipped through the large doors.

He turned back to Kerrigan, who had put away her laptop. Desperate for more time with her, Axel decided to extend the most unconventional, borderline unprofessional offer he had ever made. Facing her, he placed his imposing hand on her chair's armrest. "I'd love to show you the city sometime. I could even help you with your apartment hunt if you want."

His invitation crossed the line, but there was something about her so refreshing and stimulating that he wanted to spend more time getting to know her. Her cheeks flashed a hint of crimson. "Mr. Christensen, that's a generous offer, but my good friend Ashley is helping me. She works in the Marketing department. I've narrowed down my search to three apartments and only need to pick one and move in."

Lifting a single eyebrow, he jerked his head back. The hard, cold slap of rejection gave his ego whiplash. "All right then," he muttered through clenched teeth as he tugged at his collar again. At a loss for words, he stared at her. This was a first. Women didn't reject Axel Christensen.

He leaned in until his knee met hers, black William Fioravanti slacks brushing against soft brown skin as smooth as spun silk. "Welcome aboard, Kerrigan. You and I will get to spend lots of time together on many projects. I'm looking forward to working with you." Her refusal would spur him on to try other tactics and soon he would have access to her every day.

Shifting away in retreat from his proximity, a smile touched her lips again. Transfixed, he couldn't take his eyes off her mouth. "I'm looking forward to working with you too." Her lips moved, like an invitation to be kissed. "I'm excited about this opportunity. Thank you, Mr. Christensen."

He didn't want to let her go, but he had no good reason to hold her captive in his office.

He stood, and Kerrigan joined him. "Brenda will help you complete the necessary paperwork. If you have any questions, call me direct." He reached into his jacket, pulled out and handed her a business card. "Kerrigan, meeting you, has been a true pleasure. I'll see you again in a couple of weeks." Looking down, his eyes roamed from her breasts to her shapely calves, caressing her curvy lines again and then he extended his hand.

When his fingers wrapped around her hand for a second time, the same charge of electricity bolted through his body. He held her hand in his firm grip much longer than he should have. She didn't pull away. His eyes locked on hers searching for a shared understanding of their attraction. The warm rosy glow that kissed her cheeks gave him confirmation.

Breaking the spell, she withdrew her hand. "Thank you." Spinning on her heel, she walked away and disappeared through the large oversized oak doors. He certainly hadn't been ready for Kerrigan Mulls. The chase began from that moment.

As soon as she left, Axel made two phone calls. The first call was to Marie.

"Marie, I've just hired Kerrigan Mulls. She'll start in two weeks. I want her to attend the weekly account managers meeting. I also plan to set up one-on-one meetings with her. She has an impressive background. I'll be working with her on some special projects."

The second call made was to his father. The phone rang and as soon as his father answered, words poured out of Axel's mouth. "Have you ever met someone that you felt an immediate connection to? I've met the most extraordinary woman."

"Oh. Who is she?"

"Her name is Kerrigan Mulls. I hired her for the junior account rep position. She's gorgeous, intelligent, kind—the total package." Restless, Axel twisted in his seat, still amped up on testosterone and adrenaline. "There is something about her."

"I'm glad to hear the enthusiasm in your voice. A long time has passed since … the incident."

Axel stilled. His fingers curled tightly around the phone until his hand cramped. "I don't want to rehash the past." Kerrigan's lingering scent teased his nostrils. Inhaling the remnant vapors, the aroma sedated his mood and his grip loosened. "I have a feeling about this woman. She's going to turn my world right side up."

A jolt of excitement and apprehension hit Axel square in the gut, and then pulsed through every nerve giving him prickly stings over his entire body.

"Just be careful, son."

***

Later that evening, Kerrigan curled up on her sofa with a celebratory glass of wine. Laura Stephens would be proud. Taking the first step on her next journey, eager expectation about her new job and the possibilities that awaited her gave her hope for a new life filled with much joy and happiness. She reached for the remote, turned off the television and headed to her bedroom.

As she lay in bed, she pondered the strange and intense meeting with Axel Christensen and his unusual offer. The man, so attractive and commanding, just remembering the force of his brilliant blue eyes staring into her and feel of his leg rubbing against hers, made her heart race. Keeping her composure during the interview had been a deliberate act of self-control. His offer to escort her on an apartment search and show her the city had been a strange proposition. Perhaps he had been flirting with her and tried to find a way to spend more time with her. She laughed at her wayward thoughts. Of course, this handsome executive didn't have any interest in an average woman like her.

Kerrigan welcomed the next chapter in her life. Perhaps Axel Christensen held the key to the happiness she sought. Correction—working for A.C. Advertising would be the key, and not the man himself. She scolded herself at her misplaced thoughts feeling a sudden warm tingle that extended up her spine and ran through every limb.

CHAPTER TWO

The city pulsed around Kerrigan full of life with modern vibrancy and southern antiquities. Atlanta proved to be the place she had hoped for, a busy urban center nestled by the small-town feel of the surrounding suburbs. On her first day at work, she waited in the building's main lobby for Ashley, who had promised to show her around before she had to report in to work at nine o'clock.

Her cell phone buzzed. A text message from Ashley:

Running late. See you in ten minutes.

Already restless, sitting and waiting was the last thing she could do. Instead, she paced the lobby floor, inspecting the unique artwork that hung in the space.

***

Kerrigan didn't seem to notice the two men who exited one of the elevators on the other side of the expansive lobby. Entranced by her beauty, one man's eyes were riveted to her as he engaged in light conversation with the man next to him.

"Oh yeah, I see why you're distracted. Do you know her?"

Axel turned to Rob, his friend and owner of the studio where the agency recorded radio spots. "A little. I intend to get to know her much better."

Rob flashed a smile at Axel. "She's a knockout. Works for you?"

Axel's eyes darted back to Kerrigan. She floated gracefully from one end of the lobby to the other. "Starts today—she's the new junior account rep." She looked ravishing. The red knee-length dress that she wore yielded to the contours of her body, highlighting the delicate arch of her back, roundness of her hips and perfect behind. Her straight long hair flowed down just above her waist. Black stilettos extended her naked shapely legs. His wicked imagination seized his brain and his cock twitched. He imagined those legs wrapped around his waist as he pumped feverishly into her. He stopped himself before his body's response to his decadent thoughts went rogue.

Rob raised his brow. "The studio is ready to record this week with your blessing on two minor tweaks to the script." He lowered his voice, almost to a whisper and placed his hand on Axel's shoulder. "You gonna hit that?"

Considering Rob's question and enjoying the way her hips swayed as she paced back and forth, he cut a sideways glance at his friend and grinned. "I'm gonna hit a home run. Now give me the highlights on the spot and make it quick. I want to talk to her before she goes up to the office."

A frenzy of motion caught his eye. Axel watched as Ashley bolted through the main lobby's entrance and made her way to where Kerrigan stood.

***

"Hey, Kerri! I'm so glad you're here. Wow! Girl, you look amazing," Ashley said.

They embraced, letting out the customary jovial squeal of girlfriends reuniting.

"Thank you." In a playful gesture, Kerrigan spun around for her friend. "I'm glad I'm here too. You look fantastic yourself."

Ashley rolled her eyes and grinned. "Yeah, right. You run circles around me with only your fingernail. Look at you, you're glowing," Ashley scoffed. "How was your drive? Atlanta traffic can be hell."

"The drive was awful, but I love my new apartment. I wish we had been able to spend time together before I started today, but my old boss was determined to keep me busy until the very end."

"Not to worry. We'll make up for lost time." Ashley's mouth fell open, and her eyes grew wide as she scanned the room at a distance. "Oh my god! Whatever you do, don't move or turn around. Axel Christensen is seriously hawking you."

Her heartbeat quickened at the mere mention of his name. "Really? I hadn't noticed him. Where?"

Ashley pursed her lips and batted her eyes at Kerrigan. "Well, Mr. Christensen has certainly noticed you. He's standing over by the elevators, watching you. The man hasn't blinked yet. You would think his eyes don't have lids the way he's staring."

A rush of warmth washed over Kerrigan. "I'm sure he recognizes me from my interview. You could have told me the man was so damn hot. I was a mess in that interview."

Ashley placed her hand on her hip. "I see more than recognition on his face. Obviously, he thinks you're seriously hot too. I didn't think to mention his looks. You're such a block of ice with your anti-men rules. I didn't think you'd care." She paused. "Uh oh, he's heading this way."

Kerrigan turned slightly and saw him walking leisurely toward them. His eyes cemented on her. She blinked fast twice, testing her sight to make certain he wasn't a mirage. His swagger, bold and confident, yet not arrogant, made him that much more appealing. The gray suit he wore fit his tall muscular frame perfectly. He had on a handsome pair of expensive leather loafers. They were huge. What did they say about men with large feet? The features of his handsome face and brilliant blue eyes came into clear view as he approached.

A sudden rush of nerves invaded her and butterflies fluttered in her belly. Unleashing a man who was that damn hot on the public should be an act against the law. Why did she have this reaction? Something was wrong with her. No man had ever made her feel this way. With pining eyes, she watched his sculpted jaw line, and shapely lips move as they opened to speak.

"Good morning, Miss Turner," Axel said, greeting Ashley coolly.

Glancing at Kerrigan, Ashley shuffled her feet and twisted her mouth, a wry grin emerging. "Good morning, Mr. Christensen."

Then he turned his full attention to Kerrigan. Moving closer, he towered over her and looked down. He extended his hand to greet her and she accepted, placing her hand into his. An immense tingling sensation flooded her, the same feeling she experienced the first time their hands met, stinging her insides and making her lightheaded. Her breath caught as he devoured her with his eyes. Or did she imagine that? Hard and refined, his strapping body couldn't be hidden beneath the expensive suit. What did he look like without all those clothes on?

"Welcome. Good to see you again, Kerrigan." Stretching across his stone face like a fissure, a smile formed on his lips. He greeted Kerrigan warmer and friendlier than he had Ashley.

With her hand still in his, she wobbled on her feet. She'd met good-looking men and had gone out on the occasional date with a few, but Axel Christensen belonged in a league of his own.

Nerves taking control, the words in her mind refused to form on her dry lips, and she had to make a concerted effort to reply.

"Thank you. It's good to see you again, too." She finally managed to pry her hand out of his grasp.

The intensity of her attraction to him must have been visible, nearly tangible. The thought harrowing, she wondered if he noticed how she responded to him.

His hand touched the small of her back as he spoke. "I hope you had no problems getting in this morning," he said, luring her away from Ashley with a gentle nudge until they reached a secluded corner in the lobby.

Turning around to lean against the wall, she anchored herself as her legs went limp like wet spaghetti. "I've been told that rush hour traffic in Atlanta is terrible. I anticipated it."

Hovering over her, he placed his left hand against the wall beside her shoulder and leaned in close. He looked down at her, his head tilted to the side with a focused gaze. Evading his pensive stare, she glimpsed over his shoulder at Ashley who stood at a distance watching them with her mouth agape. Kerrigan's cold fingers clawed her thighs, her cheeks warmed, and she dipped her head low, embarrassed by the thought that others witnessed her attraction to Mr. Christensen.

His smoldering gaze stayed fixed to her. "Did you find an apartment and settle in?" he asked, forcing her attention back to him.

Her eyes darted up to meet his. "Yes, I did."

"Where?" he commanded, the pitch of his voice low and his question punctuated.

The hairs at the nape of her neck stood on end. "Buckhead. Do you know the area?"

"A little." Appearing to think her question over, he smiled lazily, not fully committed to the action. "My offer still stands to show you the parts of the city that I do know." His face tensed, brow furrowed and lips pressed together.

She nibbled her bottom lip. "Thank you. Maybe I'll take you up on your offer one day."

"You should." A grin split his face in two.

His heat rolled off in waves so hot she felt as if she would combust. She needed to keep the conversation focused on work. "I'm eager to get started. You won't be disappointed you hired me."

Clearing his throat, he startled her. "I have no doubt you'll make me a very happy man." His pupils dilated and his stare unwavering, danger flashed in his eyes and his words held double-edged meaning, sending a shiver up her spine. Feeling foolish, she knew the man was only being polite, and she had imagined his attraction to her.

He had been imposing, overpowering, intimidating and sexy. She backed out of his cocoon, inching away from the wall and him on unstable legs. "Ash, Ashley…I mean Miss Turner is going to show me around before I meet with Marie. Well, thanks again, Mr. Christensen."

He lowered his hand from the wall as though releasing her from his hold.

Gritting his teeth, he glared at Ashley, who stood a considerable distance away from them. "I'll see you again soon, Kerrigan." His eyes slithered down her body, and then he turned and left the two women standing there as he exited through the main lobby doors.

Ashley walked over and covered her mouth. "What the hell, Kerri? I can smell the attraction between you two. Keep your guard up around that damn man. He's dangerous, and I don't want to see you get hurt," Ashley whispered.

She blushed. "What are you talking about? You mean Mr. Christensen welcoming me?" They began walking toward the elevators.

"Yeah, well I was never welcomed like that. He was eye-fucking you from across the room. Don't be naïve. That wasn't a welcome. Girl that man is after you."

"We had a brief conversation, there's nothing more to say."

Throwing her hands up feigning surrender, Ashley released a heavy sigh. "Okay, but he had you pinned up against a wall. He stood dangerously close to you. Your exchange looked intimate. He wants you and the way you looked at him, and how hard you're denying the attraction makes me think you want him too. I thought you two would go *at* each other right here in the lobby." Ashley's strained voice bore into Kerrigan's conscious. She was caught with her wet panties down.

Rolling her eyes and tightening her hand into a ball, Kerrigan's fingernails burrowed deep into her fleshy palm. "Whatever. Can you please show me around and stop with this nonsense?" Releasing her fist, she jabbed repeatedly at the elevator's call button.

"You can press that button one hundred times, and it won't make the elevator get here any faster. You're stuck here listening to me," Ashley teased.

Her palms moistened and her mouth went parch, dry like the Sahara. "This is my first day. I want to make a good impression."

Ashley tugged at Kerrigan's arm and yanked her into the car when the elevator's doors opened. "Sure seems like you've already done more than that with Mr. Christensen."

***

Marie introduced Kerrigan to her co-workers and told her about her client accounts. She liked Marie, a stoic woman lacking the cognitive ability to appreciate a joke or the facial muscles to respond. At ten o'clock, she attended her first meeting with Marie and the other account managers across the company. They discussed high-level media plans and other details about the company's highest profile accounts. Mr. Christensen dropped in unexpectedly, surprising the group. His presence at these meetings had been a rarity given the wide-eyed stares and changed behaviors in the room the minute he appeared.

He sat in a white leather chair that lined the wall, quietly observing the group around the glass-top conference table. He didn't engage in conversation happening around the room except at her introduction. After Marie's welcoming remarks, he offered his high endorsement as a show of support for Kerrigan.

He watched her intensely throughout the meeting. She squirmed in her seat. His searing eyes tormented and teased, forcing a surge of heat through her body. He blatantly stared and didn't turn away, even when her eyes met his. Although his icy countenance didn't give away his attraction, she flushed under his steady gaze. Instead, his lips pulled taut into a fine line, the hard and practiced mug of a man making an appraisal. Perhaps the shrewd executive wanted to watch his investment, making sure he would get his money's worth.

Axel's jaw tensed, and his eyes narrowed as he checked his Blackberry throughout the meeting reading over incoming messages. Before the meeting ended at eleven thirty, he had winced, a tension-filled expression, at a message he had received. Soon after, he stood, issued a final pass at her with sterile blue eyes and stalked out.

***

At noon, Kerrigan and Ashley headed to lunch. They decided to walk to a quaint European bistro a few blocks away. Although no one would say the streets of downtown Atlanta offered the cleanest, freshest air, being outdoors would feel refreshing. Kerrigan descended in the elevator to the main lobby to wait for Ashley. When the doors opened, she spotted Mr. Christensen. He stood across the room, near the floor-to-ceiling windows, engrossed in conversation on his cell phone. As if sensing her presence, he turned and caught her eyes. He ended his call and while making his way to her, Axel was intercepted by a tall regal woman. The gawk of every male eye in the room trailed the blond, who threw her arms around Mr. Christensen's neck and pulled him into her embrace. His eyes closed, he grimaced and pushed away from the vixen. The woman grabbed his hand, and then they exited the building. An Adonis, naturally his girlfriend would be a damn Barbie. Her feelings irrational, Kerrigan couldn't help the slight twinge of disappointment and jealousy that coursed through her and the ensuing burning in her chest.

Walking briskly down the sidewalk, Ashley and Kerrigan headed to the bistro. Within minutes of arriving, they were seated. "I saw Mr. Christensen's girlfriend. She's gorgeous. He's not interested in me," Kerrigan blurted out.

"And, exactly how does that prove that he's not interested in you? You're gorgeous, too. Mr. Christensen has a different woman on his arm almost every time I see him. I doubt it's serious. Not to worry, I'm sure he can make room for one more notch," Ashley said and then chuckled. "Can you pass me a napkin?"

"Ha! I'm not interested in being a notch. That isn't what I want." She reached for the stainless steel napkin dispenser and pulled one out. "Here," she said, handing a napkin to Ashley.

"Thanks." Ashley wiped a smudge of red sauce away from the corner of her mouth. "You're interested in Mr. Christensen. No biggie. He's hot, and he digs you too. Just admit it, you're attracted to him."

She shrugged her shoulders and placed her fork down on her plate. "Okay, I'll admit I think he's blazing, but I'm not stupid. I'd never let him get close to me, and I'd never act on my feelings. I know what men like that are after."

Ashley wagged her index finger at Kerrigan. "Keep telling yourself that. I sure hope you're stronger than what I witnessed this morning. Mr. Christensen almost ate you alive."

"Like you said, he's dangerous. He has a different woman on his arm every time you see him. Why would I involve myself in that mess?"

"Because Axel Christensen is fine as hell and you can't resist him. Kerri, I've never seen you look at a man the way you looked at him this morning. You might as well have some fun on your quest for Mr. Right. I thought you were going to be open-minded and try new things. That includes men, too."

"I am being open-minded, but I didn't say I was going to be reckless."

"As long as you don't get your heart involved, getting reckless with Axel Christensen might be fun and well worth the risk," Ashley quipped.

Kerrigan shook her head and crossed her arms over her chest. "Sounds good in theory, but having fun with a man like him comes with consequences. I'd like to stay employed."

They finished lunch and headed back to the office. The rest of the afternoon went by quickly. Kerrigan had enjoyed her first day at the new job. Relocating to Atlanta proved to be a smart move, it was just what she wanted. She just had to get her lust for Mr. Christensen under control. She wanted a man who excited her and made her breathless, but she hadn't figured he would be dangerous or that he would be her new boss.

***

Six months later – January 9, 2012

She heated under his inspection. God, why does he do this to me? Kerrigan sat in the weekly account managers meeting distracted. She shifted restlessly in her seat and repeatedly checked her phone for messages that weren't there—anything to avoid the imposing glare of Mr. Christensen, who sat in one of the chairs lined against the wall, directly opposite her, staring. Since her arrival six months ago, he began attending the weekly account manager's meetings regularly, although he rarely took part. She avoided looking at him for fear she would catch his gaze. His stare revealed her predilection for lusty, hedonistic thoughts about him. Kerrigan's nipples hardened, shivers ran up her spine and fantasies flashed through her mind about his lips covering hers while he possessed her, explored and plundered her body. She couldn't control her reaction. No other man conjured up these feelings in her and they both excited and terrified her.

She maintained her composure during these meetings, except once. During one particular meeting in January, she had to excuse herself to get some air and escape his heat. The sexual tension reverberated thick and hot between them. She was certain the incident had started rumors.

The walls in the tight space seemed to be closing in on her. Mr. Christensen had been exceptionally intense that day. He sat in his regular seat and she in hers. With hooded eyes, he stared dauntlessly at her, eye-fucking her as Ashley called his penetrating gaze. His tongue swiped across his upper lip, and his greedy eyes roamed her body. Aware of his fixation on her, she kept her head down and her eyes glued to the notepad in her lap. Light beads of moisture dotted her hairline and her temperature rose under his heavy surveillance. Breathing in the small room with him there had become impossible. She stood and excused herself to avoid suffocation. Barreling down the hall, her chest heaved, and heart beat wildly. She lowered her head into her hands and rushed to the alcove at the end of the hallway. Why is this happening to me?

A few seconds later, she heard the sound of heavy footsteps tapping against the floor. With each step, the sound drew louder, nearer, and then silence—it stopped. She stilled as if that would make her invisible. She leaned against the wall, the palms of her hands splayed flush against the coolness at her sides, her head tilted back, eyes shut, ragged breaths escaped Kerrigan's parted lips. She imagined him leaning in and kissing her deeply. A warm sensation flooded her core as the intruder closed in, violating her personal space. Her body tensed and her eyes opened, alerted by a towering presence, his musky smell, pungent and invading her senses.

He placed his hands flatly on the wall on either side of her head to swathe her in his cover. His eyes filled with tenderness as he spoke. "Kerrigan, are you okay? Why did you leave so abruptly?" Pensively, he stared into her, his brow furrowed, and cold eyes now impassioned with depth and warmth that Kerrigan hadn't seen before. His brow wrinkled and jaw tightened, concern etched across his face.

She jolted at his unexpected presence, and her stomach twisted and knotted. "I … I needed some air. The room was warm, and I suddenly felt claustrophobic," she whispered, dropping her gaze to the floor. She couldn't believe Mr. Christensen was standing right there, so close to her, overwhelming her mind and violating her sanity.

"I see. Would you prefer that I don't attend these meetings?"

Terror flooded her heart. He knows! He knows I like him. "This isn't about you." She lied to him, her voice cracking and eyes moistening. Desperate to divert his suspicions, she added, "My leaving has nothing to do with you, Mr. Christensen."

Wrinkled lines formed across Axel's forehead, his eyes widened, and he jerked his head back, obviously surprised and insulted. Did he actually expect her to admit her attraction to him—that he had affected her to the point of necessary escape?

"I thought the pressure of the boss in the room might be too intimidating for you," he said. She wondered if his explanation had been camouflage, to disguise his hurt over her indifference toward him.

"That might be part of the problem," she conceded.

He smiled. Oh god! She couldn't avoid the lure of his perfectly chiseled face when he grinned liked that. Caught in his snare, she tilted her head and her eyes locked on his. She closed her eyes again and swallowed hard, quailing as her head dropped. Mortified. She had never been in a position like this before. If he had any idea about what she had been feeling and thinking, he didn't let on. Perhaps he wanted to save her from embarrassment.

He moved his left hand to her arm, holding her tenderly. She raised her head and opened her eyes, jarred by the intensity of his touch. When their flesh met, a tingling sensation swept through her, but she concealed her reaction. His impassive expression didn't hide the sensual heat behind his eyes.

"Kerrigan, I'm sorry. I know I can be intense. I'll stop attending these meetings. I've only come for you." She couldn't believe his brazenness. He winced, as though admonishing himself for the directness of his words. "I want to support you. You're the newest member of a very close, tight-knit team, and they can be resistant to change. From the beginning, I told Marie that you had management potential. Your work in the last six months is proof.

I'm promoting you to an account manager position, and I want to make sure the team knows I support your promotion. Understand?"

She cringed inwardly and then frowned. "Yes, I understand," she said quietly. "I appreciate your support and confidence in me, and offer for the promotion, but I don't want the job." Shocked disappointment plastered his face—his raised brow and parted lips were poised to speak, but then closed in silence. She looked down to escape his fiery gaze.

"Look at me, Kerrigan." She lifted her eyes at his command. He stared down at her so intensely that she trembled. She hoped he didn't notice. "Why don't you want this? You've worked so hard. You deserve the position. In less than six months, you've repaired a damaged relationship with two of our largest clients, and you've brought in four new accounts. I won't let you turn me down."

She swallowed hard again. "I, I can't, Mr. Christensen. I came here looking for a new start. I want a slower pace. I don't want the responsibility. If you want to fire me, I understand."

He said nothing for a few seconds, and then the corner of his mouth slanted upward into a smirk. "Why would I fire you? You're the best account rep here, the best rep who has ever worked with me, period. At least give the job some consideration. You and I would be working closely together on several projects. I think we'd make an excellent team. I can be intense, and you'll balance me out." He placed his right hand on his chest over his heart, offering his pledge. "The work will challenge you, but I promise the job won't be overwhelming. I'd never do that to you. The position comes with a salary increase, too. What do you say? Just think over my offer." He bit his lower lip, pausing while she pondered his proposal.

"May I have my old job back if I accept and then change my mind?"

"Yes, but I promise, you won't want your old job back. I want you by my side. I have grand things in store for us." Again, his words held more than their face value. "You're a stellar performer and we'll make great partners."

She inhaled a deep pained breath. He had only been thinking about business. The crush she had on her boss was going to jeopardize her success if she didn't get her lust under control. He's not after you. Stop listening to Ashley before you make a damn fool of yourself. A man like Axel Christensen had any number of beautiful models at his disposal, and someone like her didn't fit the mold and wouldn't hold his interest. From that moment, she decided to bury her feelings for him deep inside, vowing not to expose them again.

"Okay. You win. I'll accept the position under one condition." She paused.

"You've got my attention. What are your conditions this time?" He narrowed his eyes on her as the corners of his lips curled upward into a faint smile, perched on the edge of a full grin at pending victory.

She shook her head. "I don't need more money. You already pay me a handsome salary, and I've done okay for myself over the years. Instead, would you consider donating the extra money to some of the charities I support and volunteer some of your time? I can always use the tax deduction."

He studied her for a brief moment, and then slowly a victorious grin emerged, spreading wide and full. "See, you're already balancing me out. Your generosity and thoughtfulness is inspiring. Just tell me how to make out the checks and what I need to do to volunteer, and we've got a deal." He backed away, his hands down at his side, and his stance triumphant. "Kerrigan, you and I are going to be great together." He raised his brow. "You okay now?"

Inhaling another deep breath, she released surrendered vapors. "Yes. I'm fine," she said and then smiled. "Thank you, Mr. Christensen."

***

Later, she heard about complaints from others who were in the conference room speculating that their abrupt departure resulted from a lover's quarrel. She laughed at the ridiculous notion. Determined not to let Mr. Christensen affect her again, she was glad that he planned to stop attending those meetings. Instead, he offered to arrange private, one-on-one sessions with her, and of course, the thought of being alone with him caused her a number of sleepless nights. Private meetings might cause greater tension than the group setting, but at least she wouldn't be subject to an audience when drool oozed from the corner of her mouth.

CHAPTER THREE

August 20, 2012

Damn her. What in the hell is wrong with Kerrigan? Why is she so formal all the time? She resisted the raw, heated attraction that he knew existed between them. Axel pondered as he sat grimacing at Kerrigan beneath his bared teeth, a sneer masquerading as a grin. Her lips moved, and words came out, but his mind raced with rousing fantasies, making concentration and understanding not possible. Energized by her presence, his temperature rose, blood raced through his veins and his throat tightened. He knew just what he would do if he ever got the chance. *I'd have her screaming my name at the top of her lungs.* Axel respected her mind, admired her professional skills, but being so close to her drove him crazy, and the red-blooded male part of himself throbbed with desire. *I'd spread her legs so wide and pound her so good that…* Blinking hard twice, he couldn't focus on anything she said. His mind raced, sexual fantasies controlling his brain kept him in a perpetual daydream.

He lifted her blouse and his eyes widened, discovering her perfectly round bosom bouncing freely. Skilled fingers circling her round breasts, he coaxed them to swell and then slowly descended his watering mouth onto a hard nipple.

She squinted, her brow wrinkling as she sat at the conference table in his office gaping at him. "Uh, um. Mr. Christensen." She paused. "What do you think about the proposal? Would you like … do you … should I make plans to meet with the McBride Group?" she stammered timidly, ripping Axel from his salacious thoughts.

Tugging at the tight collar around his neck to ease his rough breathing, his stomach hardened. He hoped she didn't realize that he wasn't paying attention to whatever she had been saying.

A few more moments of awkward silence passed before the meaning of her words registered in his cerebral cortex. He placed his elbow on the smooth wooden table and gripped his temples between his index finger and thumb.

"What?" he rasped, her words still catching up to him. "Yeah, I'll need time to think it over, Kerrigan. I want to play my cards just right. The McBride account is difficult." Rubbing the back of his neck, he released a hard breath and lowered his voice. "I honestly didn't think we'd reach this stage. You shouldn't be surprised if we don't win this one. I don't want you to be upset over this account." He lowered his hand and patted her forearm, leaving his hand to rest there. A prickly sensation greeted his touch and radiated to his spine. "This isn't a reflection of your capabilities. I've pitched this guy before. He's tough, a bit intense." He moved in closer, a mixture of a floral fragrance and her natural scent flooded his nostrils. "I know you're capable of putting up your defenses against a man even more intense than this one, aren't you?"

Slipping her arm out of his hand, she slinked away from the table. Even her fair caramel skin tone couldn't hide the red glow that kissed her cheeks. Although he was the owner of the agency and her boss, she'd be dead wrong to think he wasn't interested or that he wouldn't act on his attraction.

Reclining in his seat, he slowly stroked his chin. "I believe you can command any man to his knees to do your bidding, can't you?"

Blinking rapidly, she stilled. "I … I guess so." Her voice cracked.

Axel enjoyed watching her fluster, her beautiful face contorting with emotion. He wondered what she was thinking now.

Smirking at her humble reaction, he twisted his lips. "Hmm. You're being modest. I recall you took over the Danvers account when Megan and Claire couldn't handle the client. They were beside themselves. Your finesse in managing the account put them both to shame. That makes you a rare treasure." Raising his brow, his eyes cascaded gingerly from hers, down to her bosom and back up. "You're oblivious to the effect you have on others. I'm sure glad you work for me and not for one of my competitors because even I'm not immune to you." He paused, and then the ends of his mouth curved upward. "I think you could get me to do almost anything."

Kerrigan blushed again. His remark an open invitation, he expected her to flirt back. Silence screamed loudly, the dull hum of the laser printer on his desk making the only sound in the room.

She offered her crescent smile, bright and beaming like the moon. "Thank you Mr. Christensen. It's good to know I'm appreciated." Avoiding his gaze, her eyes focused on her fidgety, manicured hands resting in her lap.

He spent the last six months in misery day-in and day-out. Sexy, curvaceous and exotically beautiful, Kerrigan sashayed about the office tempting his masculine restraint. On more than one occasion, he had invited her out to dinner under the guise of an office gathering only to be rejected. She always gave the excuse of volunteering as a tutor at some school as her out.

Rubbing his furrowed eyebrows, he assessed her with his unwavering stare. He leaned back in his chair until it teetered on two legs and then brought it down slowly.

This time he spoke to her with authority. "You and I will entertain McBride. You know, show him a good time and eventually win him over. I want you to work with the creative team and turn that proposal into a slick presentation." He paused, ran his hand through his thick hair and then stood.

Pacing the long edge of the table across from Kerrigan, his fingertips glided along the cold surface. He always thought best on his feet and he needed all the brainpower possible, making up his plan on the spur as words spilled from his lips. "We'll need time to review and prep before we meet with McBride. I'm going to schedule a few meetings for you and me over the next few weeks. We'll spend as much time together as it takes to work through the details of the presentation."

Her nervous eyes fluttered following his footsteps. "We'll start this week. Brenda will send the meeting schedule to you once she confirms with McBride. Kerrigan, make sure you're available this Wednesday evening for our first meeting. We'll leave from here at seven o'clock. I'll drive." He halted his steps and turned. "Oh, and from now on, call me Axel. As closely as we work together, it seems odd that you call me Mr. Christensen." He sat down again, positioning himself close to her.

Repeatedly twirling her long strand of pearls around delicate piano fingers, her eyes darted from him to the closed door on the other side of the room.

"Any questions?" he asked. Landing on his, her eyes grew large, again.

Her restless fingers were joined by the incessant swing of her crossed leg, bouncing. "Uh, no Mr. Christen … I mean, Axel," she stammered.

She was uncomfortable having to address him by his first name, but she'd get used to it. "That's all, Kerrigan. I'm glad we're working together on this project. See you later."

Unsteady on her feet, she stood. He reached out and grabbed her wrist to help her stabilize. Almost holding her hand, the simple touch made his stomach roll.

"Your balance seemed a little off kilter when you got up. You okay?"

She swallowed hard. "Um, yes … yes, thank you." Sputtering her words again, she broke free from his grasp and whipped pass him where he sat. Her stilettos tapped fiercely against the hardwood as her gait quickened. "Goodbye," she said, rubbing the wrist where he held her and then she was gone.

***

Axel did something to Kerrigan, making her feel both terrified and exhilarated. Besides their private one-on-one meetings, she usually worked as part of a larger team on projects where he was involved. This would be the first time they would work together exclusively. The thought made her nervous.

Her legs carried her back to her office as fast as they could move. Jittery and shaken after the encounter, she sat down at her computer and started on the McBride presentation. She replayed his words in her head over, and over, again. An incredibly smart man, Axel's suggestive phrases weren't merely a poor choice of words strung together haphazardly. What did they mean exactly?

The ping of an incoming email caught her attention disrupting her thoughts—an invitation to lunch the following day and to the Wednesday evening meeting. She was amazed at how quickly Axel Christensen made things happen.

Not even five minutes had passed before Ashley knocked and peered through the door. Kerrigan waved her in. After closing the door behind her, Ashley grinned widely as she took a seat across from her desk.

"So, what happened? Mr. Christensen had you in there for quite a while today. Kind of sent some of the groupies into a heated frenzy," Ashley smirked.

Kerrigan rolled her eyes. "You're probably the leader of said frenzy. We met about the McBride account. Mr. Chris … I mean Axel was absolutely professional. He even paid me a compliment," she defended.

"Axel? You've always called him Mr. Christensen. Since when did you two become so chummy that your vocabulary was upgraded, to first name basis? That must have been some compliment," Ashley teased.

"Cut it out, Ash! Seriously, I mean it. He's giving me a chance to prove myself in this new role. He insisted that I call him Axel since we'll be working together on this account, spending lots of time with McBride himself. I'm really nervous about the whole thing, and I could use your support."

Ashley leaned forward, and a serious expression took hold of her. "Two things–One, you'll do a terrific job. You got this promotion because you have the skills, have worked hard, and most importantly, you deserve the job because you get results. Two, Axel Christensen has a thing for you, and that's what you should be nervous about, Kerri. I'm not the only one who's noticed. There's a buzz in the office. Haven't you seen the way he looks at you? Are you blind?" Ashley pursed her lips and raised her brow. "The man practically salivates in meetings when you're in the room. He stares at you as though you're a steak and he's a starving man. If I were you, I'd get Axel to nail me good," Ashley quipped.

She felt herself warm, but she managed to stave off a full-on blush. "Ash! Oh my god! Just stop. Please. That's inappropriate. I don't care about the office buzz. Hasn't the thought occurred to anyone he's watching me closely because he's been assessing my performance?"

"He's assessing something," Ashley muttered under her breath.

Kerrigan released a heavy sigh and rolled her eyes again. "He wants to make sure he made the right decision by giving me this promotion. That's all, nothing more. Here, look at this." She pushed the torn piece of paper across the desk to Ashley.

"What's this?" Ashley looked at the newspaper clipping, her lips twisted into a frown.

"That's an article in today's paper about A.C. Advertising. They refer to Axel as the millionaire playboy. See, I know all about his reputation. Now please, I have work to do. I'll talk to you later." She hoped that was enough to get Ashley off her back for the rest of the day, at least. She already had too much to process after the intense meeting with him.

Ashley rose to leave, holding a laugh back. "Okay. I'm sorry, but you know I call it as I see it. That article doesn't prove you're not into him. Like I said before, he's on the prowl for you and men like that usually get what they want. I hope you remember my theory the first time he makes a move on you. Nah, you probably won't. You'll be too dazed and breathless to think about little old me in the heat of the moment."

Ashley had more experienced with men and thought her naïve. Kerrigan valued her advice, but sometimes she could be over the top. She couldn't tell Ashley about Axel's suggestive remarks during their meeting.

Ashley tossed her hair over her shoulder and closed the door behind her. A second later, she pushed her way back through the door. One hand mounted her hip, and the other held up high halted the air. "Let me know when you're ready for the birds and bees conversation. You need to be prepared for a man like that." Kerrigan shook her head at Ashley's whispered remark.

Snickering and still standing in Kerrigan's doorway, Ashley pivoted, staring at someone in the hall. A clear view of Ashley's face, Kerrigan saw her turn ashen gray. The rumble of a deep voice could be heard from the hall.

Ashley blushed and greeted him. "Oh! Hello Mr. Christensen," she said in a shaky high-pitched voice. Ashley smiled, but based on her ghastly expression, he must not have returned the gesture kindly. "Miss Turner." Even the sterile sound of his voice made Kerrigan's belly flutter. Ashley twisted her lips, glanced at Kerrigan, and then scampered away.

The sting of tears burned behind Kerrigan's eyes. Others in the office thought she didn't deserve the account manager position—that Axel's infatuation with her had led to her promotion. On some level, she knew they shared a strong mutual attraction. Although she did everything to ignore her desire, he made her skittish whenever he was near. Why couldn't she shake this feeling, shake this man out of her brain?

Pushing thoughts about Axel aside, she became more determined than ever to prove to herself that she deserved her new job. She had spent the past year busting her ass, and she was infuriated that others thought she was promoted for reasons other than her hard work and skill. Maybe if she helped land the McBride account she'd earn the respect of her co-workers.

About to leave for the day, her mouse hovered over the exit button on her email application when an incoming email caught her eye. It was from Axel himself, not Brenda his assistant.

She could count on one hand how many email messages had come directly from him to her in the past year–this one. The subject was short and to the point. She opened the message with nervous anticipation.

Monday, August 20
To: Kerrigan Mulls
From: Axel Christensen
Subject: Lunch Tomorrow
Kerrigan,
I hope you had a productive day. I know you've been working hard on the McBride presentation, but not too hard, I hope. I'm eager to see it tomorrow. It will be good for us to spend time together to get acquainted. We need to have good chemistry as we pitch. I'll stop by your office around Noon. I should have you back by 2:00 p.m. I'm looking forward to seeing you.
Axel Christensen
President and Chief Executive Officer
A.C. Advertising

The thought of a two-hour lunch with Axel Christensen made her stomach twist. *What can we possibly discuss for two hours?* Taking a deep breath, she shut down her computer. These problems could wait for the next day and it would be best to leave them for tomorrow.

The office was empty now. Nearly seven thirty in the evening, everyone else in the department had gone home. Grabbing her handbag, Kerrigan headed toward the door and turned out the light. She spun around and took a step back to look at her desk one last time making sure she had remembered her cell phone. It wasn't on her desk, which meant she had already put in her handbag. Whirling around to make her way out, she slammed straight into a solid brick mass, colliding into him.

Axel must have been standing at her door silently observing her. He had removed his jacket and the top two buttons of his white dress shirt were undone. The palms of her hands landed squarely onto his rock-hard pecks and she tried to steady herself. She could feel the peaks and valleys of his well-defined chest through the thin material of his shirt.

She stepped back abruptly, nearly stumbling to a fall. He caught her by the small of her waist and pulled her closer to him to prevent her inevitable backwards tumble. Their bodies were flush, her breasts pressed firmly against his chest. Holding her in a tight, protective embrace, his strong arms locked her in place against him. She was dizzy and breathless. He looked down at her with impassioned eyes.

"Ah! Mr. Christensen, I mean, Axel. I am sorry. I … I didn't see you, standing there." She lowered her head down, unable to meet his eyes.

A warm sensation swept over her when she realized that he was still holding her close and hadn't made a motion to release her. She startled when she felt Axel's growing bulge press firmly against her stomach. He didn't attempt to push her away. Breaking his grip, she pulled out of his clutch.

He looked down at her with hooded eyes and spoke softly, almost seductively. "It's okay. No harm was done. I didn't mean to startle you. I was leaving, saw your light on, and I thought I'd escort you out. That's the least I can do since I'm going to work you so hard over the next few weeks."

His words were unnerving. She blushed at the thought. She was clearly out of line and apparently, her mind wandered straight to the gutter whenever he was near.

"That's kind of you. Thank you. Again, I apologize."

"Forget it. Your bumping into me isn't the worst thing that could happen. Let's go."

She analyzed his word choice again. Was it a compliment or something more? She dismissed the latter.

They were walking out of the building when he paused. "I've got to lock up since we're the last ones here. Where's your car?"

"It's on the bottom level. Really, I'll be fine. You don't have to escort me the whole way."

"Of course I do. You aren't walking to your car alone on other evenings when you work late, are you? I don't want anything happening to you. I want you safe." He said and continued locking the door to the office suite.

She shifted on her feet and stepped back, putting some distance between them. "Usually, Kevin, one of the security officers, offers to walk with me."

He frowned. "Oh, I'll bet he does," he muttered under his breath.

They walked to the parking deck elevator and waited for the doors to open. Once they were inside, she squirmed as his eyes roamed up and down her body. After what felt like an eternity, the elevator came to a halt, the doors opened slowly, and as though she was a caged bird freed, she nearly flew out.

"Thanks for seeing me off safely, Mr. Christensen … Axel. My car is right there." She pointed toward her vehicle.

"Any time, Kerrigan. I'm looking forward to lunch tomorrow."

Holding the elevator doors open, he watched until she was safely inside her car.

At home, Kerrigan sat at her dining room table, toying with the food on her plate and replaying the events of their latest encounter in her head. There was no mistaking Axel's raging erection, the scintillating magnetism between them when they touched as he held her close in the office, or the lusty gaze in his eyes as they raked up and down her body in the elevator. She was torn and confused, harrowed by the thought that Axel found her attractive, yet he excited her, and she felt alive.

***

Tuesday, August 21

Kerrigan arrived at the office early the next morning to put final touches on the McBride presentation. The office buzzed with news that she was working directly with Mr. Christensen on the McBride account. Rich poked his head into her office. He was one of the account reps on her team who had hit on her a few times only to be rejected because she wasn't interested. She was done dating jerks and losers just because she had nothing planned, on a lonely Friday evening.

The slight lisp of his nasally voice assaulted her eardrums like nails on a chalkboard. "I heard you're working solo with Christensen on the McBride project. He's a sly one. If only I had more clout and a hefty bank account." His clammy skin, crooked nose and long skinny body reminded her of the snake that he was, and her stomach churned. He winked, and then slithered off.

She didn't like what Rich was insinuating. She ignored him and returned to her work. Soon, it would be time for lunch with Axel and the minutes were slipping away. Another co-worker came into her office at eleven thirty. It seemed that everyone had inappropriate remarks to share today. This time it was Megan's turn.

Megan hustled in uninvited, leaning against her desk. "It must be nice to be the boss' favorite. I'd give anything to work directly with Mr. Christensen one-on-one. You're a lucky girl. It must be tempting being that close to him."

"Megan, I have no idea what you're talking about. I'm nobody's favorite. Mr. Christensen likes how I handle our difficult clients. That's not luck, that's a skill. He's the boss, and I'm simply doing my job, nothing more. I have a few more minutes before my lunch meeting, and I need to finish my presentation."

Megan huffed, jerked her shoulders back and scampered out.

***

Precisely at Noon, Axel appeared in her doorway, watching her furtively. He thought about how easily he could rip open her snug blue blouse and free her breasts. He would knead her perfect mounds in his hands before taking one into his mouth to lick and suck, and drive her insane.

"Mmm." He let out a small groan as his thoughts ran wild.

Swiveling around in her office chair with her hand to her chest, "Ah!" she gasped loudly.

"Ready?"

"Oh! Hello, Mr. Christensen, I didn't see you, standing there. I'm ready. I just printed copies for us to review."

"Good. I figured both of us could use some fresh air. Care to walk?"

"Sure. That sounds great."

She stood and made her way toward the doorway, her hair cascading over one shoulder. Today, she had worn it straight. He stood steadfast. His heart nearly stopped. Even with the slightest movement, her breasts bounced. Wrapped in the tight black skirt she wore, her hips swayed rhythmically. Full delicious lips and big round hazel eyes stared widely back at him. He didn't hide his appreciation. Around her, he didn't feel like the cold, young successful CEO that everyone had pegged him to be. He was a wanton man full of carnal need entranced by the object of his desire. Leaning against the doorframe, heavy lids covering his eyes and his bottom lip tucked beneath his top row of teeth, he drank in every inch of her sexy curvaceous frame with his eyes.

The hunger in her eyes could not be mistaken—this was no one-sided attraction. Her round eyes scaled the length of his body and then she bit down on her bottom lip, mimicking him. Her lips parted, and her breathing quickened into a quiet pant. He had never seen her react that way to him before. Their eyes locked in the heated exchange that lasted far longer than was appropriate and no words were spoken between them. Axel raised his brow, slowly pursed his lips and gave a slight nod, an expression and gesture evincing his recognition of her attraction to him and a silent challenge daring her to explore it. She swallowed hard and looked away, breaking their trance. Game on.

"I'll meet you in the lobby in ten minutes."

"Sure, okay," She murmured back, keeping her gaze locked on a folder on her desk.

***

Axel entered the executive suite like a bolt of lightning, and flashed pass Brenda. "I don't want to be disturbed under any circumstances."

Hurrying into his office, he slammed and locked the door behind him, and made his way to his desk. Anxious fingers found their way to his groin. He unzipped his slacks and released his cock, explicit images of Kerrigan running through his head—her delicious caramel body splayed naked, her legs spread wide, and her breasts bouncing wildly as he pumped hard and deep into her. He stroked himself, pulling and tugging until he found his release. *Kerrigan. God! She's killing me.* He was careful, not to soil his pants. After the deed, he stepped into his private bathroom, to clean up.

Still hard, the damn thing wouldn't go down. *Shit!* Running his hand up and down his shaft again, he had reached near climax when suddenly the intercom on his office phone sounded.

He answered through gritted teeth, his breathing harsh. "What do you need, Brenda?"

"Sir, I know you said not to disturb you, but Kerrigan Mulls is here. She's been waiting in the main lobby for twenty minutes."

Her timing couldn't be better, or worse. *Invite her in, fuck her brains out and be done, get her out of my system.* He imagined her expression if he were to bring her into his office while he held his cock in his hand and explained what he wanted to do. The coy game she would play, batting those big round eyes and flaunting that sexy body, acting the part of the innocent when she was deliberately torturing him—the seductress. The problem—he wanted more than a quick lay. He actually liked her. *Shit!*

"Brenda, please ask her to wait in the main lobby downstairs. I'll be down soon," he barked.

"Okay, sir. I'll let her know."

At least the interruption tamed his erection. Brenda interrupting him during masturbation was the equivalent to his mother catching him yanking off to a dirty magazine—an easy turn off.

His second act not fully carried out, he had no choice but to face her. With the intensity between them mounting, he was more determined than ever to break her.

CHAPTER FOUR

Tuesday, August 21, 2012

Five minutes later, Axel appeared in the lobby, to find Kerrigan standing at the large floor-to-ceiling windows, peering out at the city as he walked up and stood next to her. Aware of his presence, she turned to greet him.

"Sorry about disappearing. I had to take care of something. You ready?" He kept his voice smooth and calm, hoping his anxiety didn't come across. He had waited for such a long time, to get her alone and away from the office.

"Yes. I'm ready."

He tugged her elbow playfully. "Great. It's such a beautiful day out. You might have to convince me to come back. Come on, let's go."

She smiled back, and her tight shoulders relaxed. "Well, you're the boss. If you decide to play hooky, I can't stop you," she said with an effervescent tone like bubbles overflowing from a champagne glass.

"No, you probably couldn't stop me, but I'd take you with me. I need a partner in crime if I'm going to play hooky. Besides, I think we could have a lot of fun together."

Her lips stretched into a beam. "Just in case this is a test, you should know that I'd never take advantage of company time."

"I think I need to keep you close to me at all times. You'll keep me honest."

He led them to a park nestled between an old office building and a wooded area. When they arrived, he pulled out his cell phone.

"We're here. Yes, right now. Thanks," he said to the person on the other end of the call.

He turned and penetrated her with his heavy gaze. "I thought we'd enjoy lunch in the park. Food is on the way. Okay with you?" He studied her face.

Her eyes sparkled like stars in the Milky Way. "Yes. This is perfect weather. I love being outdoors."

He stretched out his arms wide, enjoying the rays of sunlight. "Great."

They walked along the tree-lined cobblestone pathway to a remote section of the park where tables and benches were arranged. A stonewall separated the area from an open green space, making it secluded and intimate. A wide variety of plants and mums painted in various shades of pink, white, yellow, red and purple lined the top of the wall, adding height for privacy. The skyline was a panorama painted with tall skyscrapers made of metal and glass stretching toward the stratosphere. The sounds of urban life were muffled in the distance. A brilliant afternoon sun played peek-a-boo in the bright blue sky behind fluffy white clouds. Freshly cut lawn and the sweet aroma of a botanical haven permeated their senses.

He led them to a garden table in the secluded seating area of the park. He towered behind her as he pulled out her chair, brushing his nose against her soft hair. Closing his eyes, he inhaled the floral fragrance that was uniquely hers. His heart raced in his chest, and his mouth became dry.

After she had sat, he maneuvered his chair to the side of the table, sitting more closely to her. Two copies of the McBride presentation in hand, she passed one to him. The light graze of her fingers sent a cold chill up his spine. Flipping through the pages of his copy, he paused as he read them over. A slow, easy smile crept onto his lips.

"Kerrigan, this is amazing. You're amazing. It's brilliant how you've played into McBride's love of sport fishing with the campaign's theme. I think you should present, not me. I know the man quite well. He'll respond much better to an intelligent, beautiful woman than he would respond to me."

"You're kind, but I've never pitched anything this big before. Are you sure you want me to do it?"

He captured her eyes with his and held her gaze. His reply was slow. Husky. Deliberate. "I've never been more certain of anything. I want you."

Cheeks reddening, she blinked rapidly and twisted her fidgety hands together on the table.

"Besides, I'll be there supporting you. You have exceptional talent and tremendous potential. This is good for your growth as an account manager. I believe in you. I'll always be there for you."

Her crossed leg bounced up and down in a jerky movement. "Mr. Christensen … Axel, thanks for your support and belief in me. This is an exciting opportunity. I won't let you down." Her voice pitched.

Placing his hand on hers, he stroked her gently. "You're welcome. It's well deserved, and you'll be great. Now that business is out of the way, we can talk about other things."

With eyes riveted on his hand resting on hers, she bounced her leg more frantically. He knew this simple act would affect her, but he also sensed her apprehension.

He lifted his hand away. "For starters, I thought we agreed that you'd call me Axel. Mr. Christensen sounds too formal. I want to you be comfortable with me."

"Sorry. Old habits die hard." A strong wind blew wisps of her long hair across her face.

"Good," he said, the thin line across his face fading into a smile.

Moments later, a rustling sound drew Axel's attention. The bearded deliveryman approached carrying a white canvas tote and plastic bag. He placed sandwiches and bottles of water on the table and left after Axel tipped and thanked him.

"Now tell me, you work so hard, what do you do for fun?"

She took a swig of water. "Oh. I'm truly boring, actually. I enjoy reading a good book. I love outdoor activities like hiking, boating and biking. There's something magical about being under the open sky. Sometimes, I catch a concert or play—pretty typical stuff."

"There's nothing boring about you. I love the outdoors too. I mostly go hiking or bike. What about your friends? You didn't mention doing things with them." He wondered if Kerrigan had a boyfriend or if she was seeing anyone.

She twirled a long strand of hair between nervous fingers. "I'm sort of a loner. I have a few close friends, Ashley for one. She likes to hang out at bars and clubs, but that just isn't my scene. I go to provide moral support mostly, and usually I'm the designated driver. I'm not into drunken men hitting on me."

"Yeah, bars and clubs can be obnoxious. I'm not into drunken men hitting on me either." He joked, trying to break the tension. She giggled. "I'm somewhat of a loner too. I prefer to spend quality time with people that mean something to me. That's a very short list." He paused, looking into her eyes. "You'd make that list, Kerrigan."

"The newspaper sure makes it seem like you're out clubbing every night and charming the ladies," she said.

Troubled by the accusation, his smile inverted, and his eyebrows made a sharp downward arrow.

He shook his head. "You shouldn't believe everything you read. The thought of me charming the ladies as you put it, does that bother you?"

"Why should that bother me? What you do in your personal life is none of my business." She shrugged her shoulders unconvincingly.

He stared directly into her eyes, without as much as a smile. "You brought up the women, so I thought they meant something to you. Just to be clear, the media reports shouldn't upset you, especially because they aren't true." She dared to go down that road with him, and he wasn't backing off now. "You should know that I'm a one-woman man, despite what you may have heard or read or think you know about me."

"Good to know," she said. She was wise to limit her reply and not to goad him further.

"Is that so?" His brow raised, he bit into his sandwich and chewed slowly.

"Yes. I can only imagine how exhausted you would be living up to that reputation. I'm relieved to know that my boss is more focused than the newspaper reports."

The corners of his lips twisted into a smirk. She always reminded him of his position. "I'm glad to relieve you of your worry. Now that we've established the truth, we can move on to more interesting topics. I enjoy learning new things about my employees." *Take that.*

The rest of their chat had been easy. Two o'clock came, and then it went—they would be late getting back to the office. He enjoyed her company, and learning that they shared similar tastes, interests, likes and dislikes.

"After graduating from business school, I had no idea what I wanted to do with my life," he said.

She nodded in agreement. "Me either."

"I interned at an agency in New York for six months, and I loved it."

"I interned at an agency after college, too. The creative energy and excitement of the hustle and bustle won me over too." A smile touched her eyes. "My first real gig was in New York."

He wrinkled his forehead. "Why did you leave the city?" he asked.

"The pace got old. Plus, I received an offer I couldn't refuse—tripled my salary and moved to Texas where the cost of living was much better. Besides, I landed the internship thanks to one of my brother's connections. In some way, I wanted to prove to my family that could make it on my own. They weren't thrilled with my career choice."

"That's why I started the agency. I didn't want my father's money. I wanted to achieve success on my own terms and of my own merit. I've always believed in hard work, but I play hard too."

"So, you're just a regular hardworking Joe?" She teased, the smile in her voice chiming like a song.

He cocked his head to one side. "I'm as regular as they come—just a little more interesting, I hope."

Axel was undoubtedly flirting. He hoped that making her realize how down-to-earth he was would ease her antsy jitters and anxiety whenever they were together.

This was a good start. He enjoyed spending one-on-one time with Kerrigan, getting to know her personally. Although he could spend all afternoon with her, he knew the afternoon had to end.

"Thank you for indulging me in a game of hooky this afternoon. Better get you back to the office. I'd hate your reputation to be smeared by the likes of me. You might be mistaken as the lady I'm keeping company with," he teased, trying to gauge her reaction.

Shifting in her seat, Kerrigan raised one eyebrow and rubbed her nose. "I didn't mean to insult you." Her voice was soft and meek.

"It's disappointing that I have this reputation. It's quite opposite of the man I am. I want so much more," he said.

"Aw, the plight of the highly sought, eligible bachelor," she sneered.

He stood and held out his hand to help her up. "It's too bad that I'm not highly sought by one woman I want."

She placed her hand in his, and he helped her up from the chair. Her touch surprised him, not expecting the rush of warmth that started in his hand, moved up his arm, and then radiated through his torso and down to his feet. They walked back through the park quietly neither saying a word. When they neared the front of the building, he slowed his pace, prolonging their time together.

Facing forward, he observed her with a furtive glance from the corner of his eye. "I'm a bachelor but, not by choice. I've been waiting for the right woman to come along so I can show her what I'm made of, whom I am and how good things can be with me."

"I'm sure you'll find your special lady someday," she said.

He stopped, gently grabbing her by the forearm and she whirled around to face him. He peered into her eyes. "I already have, but she'll take some convincing. She keeps barriers between us. Kerrigan, do you have any idea how I can get her to trust me, open up to me?"

His words landed perfectly as if he were an arrow and she the dartboard. Bulls-eye.

"Sounds as if you need a healthy dose of patience. Give her time to learn to trust you," she said.

He released her arm. Hope was a lighter load than the uncertainty that he had carried all these months. "Hmm. That is good advice. Although I'm not a patient man, especially when I know what I want." He glanced back down at her.

"If you're not willing to wait for her, she must not be very special to you."

He caught her eyes again. "She's incredibly special to me. Of course, I want things to move along faster, but I know she's afraid. What are you afraid of, Kerrigan?" *Shit.* The question blurted out.

She gasped and stepped back. "Excuse me?"

His heart hammered in his chest. "I, I meant … your womanly insights might be helpful," he stammered. "What would make you afraid to explore your feelings?"

"That's a topic for another day." She rested her fanned hand on her chest at the base of her throat.

"I'll hold you to that. So, have you written any pages in your new chapter? Are you finding everything you had come here looking for?"

She shrugged her shoulders. "I'm learning that writing a new chapter takes time. I've found some things I was looking for, and well others … not so much." Her eyes sank.

"Then we'll definitely have to do this again. Maybe we can find a way to get you everything you're looking for, and you can give me your perspective on what might make a woman afraid to explore her feelings."

He held the door open for her. The light in her eyes flickered out, and they glossed over, her expression downcast. He wasn't sure if his directness had upset her, but her mood passed in an instant. As they entered the building, she turned and flashed him with the beaming glow of her gentle smile. Adrenaline pumped through his system and his heart fluttered.

"Thank you for lunch. I'll practice delivering the presentation."

"Kerrigan, I enjoyed your company. We'll do lunch again soon. Don't forget about tomorrow evening. Give me your cell phone number in case I need to reach you. I'll dial you now, and then you'll have my number too. We'll leave here at seven. Wear something comfortable like jeans. We'll have fun."

After they had exchanged phone numbers, she pivoted on her heel, heading toward the elevator. Giving him a sideways glance, she tossed words at him over her shoulder. "Thanks again for lunch."

Watching her slink from his view, she was as lovely, going and coming, the sway of her hips rekindling memories of his earlier predicament and he was back where he started.

***

Kerrigan unlocked her front door and rushed inside. Her thoughts returned to her conversation at lunch with Axel. Who was this mystery woman? He could have any woman he wanted. She had seen some of them, beautiful models, tall blonds and brunettes—that was the kind of woman who would steal his heart. The conversation made her uncomfortable, and although she knew she had no right to be, she was angry. He had confessed his interest in someone else and wanted her help to get into the psyche of his mystery woman. She knew she needed to abandon any silly romantic notions she had about him.

She had a long day and still had lots to do. She thought about what she should wear to work the next day, especially for the client meeting with Harris McBride that evening. She would have to bring a change of clothes since Axel had told her to wear jeans. She packed black skinny jeans, a shimmery red blouse and ballerina flats. What would he think of her outfit? She reminded herself that he was a dangerous proposition to be avoided at all costs. What he thought didn't matter.

After she had eaten dinner, she called her mother for a quick chat.

"How are you sweetie?"

"I'm good. How are you? How's dad?"

"Oh, we're both fine. Nothing new on this end. Are you enjoying your new job?"

She wasn't about to reveal her secret crush on the boss. Other than the strange situation with Axel, she was happy about the move to Atlanta, the city was turning out to be exactly what she hoped Atlanta offered—well, almost.

"I'm preparing for my first major presentation. I'm going out with the client tomorrow evening. I'm nervous about our meeting. I heard the guy is a jerk."

"You'll be fine. Are you going alone?"

She couldn't help grinning like an idiot whenever she thought about him. "No, I'm going with the CEO of my company. The same man who hired and promoted me, so no pressure, right?" She was glad her mother couldn't see her face.

"That's fantastic honey! He obviously trusts you. Where are you taking your client? To a dinner?"

"Not exactly. Axel hasn't told me where we're going, but he said I should wear jeans." She liked saying his name and with her mom, she could say his name in an unassuming way.

"Axel?"

"Oh. Sorry. Axel Christensen. That's my boss' name."

"He's got an odd name. Well, just be you. I know you'll do an outstanding job."

"Thanks mom. Axel is very encouraging. He's a great guy." She hadn't realized that the words leaped from her lips with such enthusiasm until they were spoken. Her mother didn't detect anything unusual.

They talked a short while longer about her dad and brother before hanging up. She climbed into bed and still feeling chatty, she called Ashley, to tell her about the lunch meeting with Axel.

"I told you he's after you," Ashley said, after Kerrigan had described how suggestive Axel had been.

Kerrigan rolled her eyes. "He's just a flirt and nothing more."

"Uh huh. You have a crush on him. He's ridiculously attractive, more than attractive. You could do a lot worse than him."

She rolled onto her stomach and propped herself up on her elbows. "You know I think he's hot, but I know better. He's dangerous, even you agree. Men like Axel aren't interested in women like me for the long haul and I'm not interested in being the office fling. Ash, Axel is just a flirt, that's all."

"What if he seriously likes you? What if all his talk about finding the right woman was about you? The man can't keep his eyes off you. He finds reasons to be around you. Others have noticed too. Hmm … private lunches and one-on-one meetings. Sounds suspect to me."

Kerrigan was reminded of both Rich's and Megan's remarks. People in the office had been talking.

"Really? Our meetings are about the McBride account," Kerrigan replied sarcastically.

"Then why is he using your meeting time to talk about romance? Word on the street says that he's trying to get you in bed or that you're already sleeping together."

Angered, Kerrigan turned and sat straight up. "What? That's outrageous! I'm working with him, and that doesn't mean we're sleeping together." She fumed.

"I know that, and of course, I defend you, but that doesn't stop the gossips. If I were you, I wouldn't worry about the rumors." Ashley's soothing tone eased Kerrigan's anger. "I'd worry about finding out Axel's motives. Is he playing a game or is he serious about you?"

She closed her eyes and placed her head into her hands. "Oh, I'm so confused. Honestly, I do like him, but I know what he's after and I don't do the casual sex thing."

"I hear you, but if you do decide to put a little cream in your coffee, I won't be mad at you. Axel is one hell of a specimen." Ashley let out a garish laugh, melting Kerrigan's tension.

They both giggled like silly teenagers, and then ended the conversation. Soon afterward, Kerrigan turned in to bed, thinking about her conversation with Axel that afternoon. Perhaps Ashley was right. Maybe he had been finding or creating reasons to get her alone. She didn't let the thought linger too long before drifting off to sleep.

CHAPTER FIVE

Wednesday, August 22

Kerrigan was on the edge about the meeting with McBride that evening. All day she had been thinking about what she should and shouldn't say. Although this wasn't the formal pitch, she knew that developing a positive relationship with McBride was critical. Brenda had sent her an email on Axel's behalf reminding her that he would meet her at seven o'clock in the lobby. She was glad that they were meeting so late. Everyone would be gone by then. Someone seeing them leave together was the last thing she needed. The rumor mill factory would go into overdrive.

At six thirty, she went to change into her jeans and blouse, and then headed to the lobby. When she arrived, Axel was already there waiting. The butterflies in her belly fluttered at the sight of him. She had never seen Axel dressed so casually. He sported dark, designer denim, a white button down shirt and stylish sporty loafers. *Damn! He's fine as hell.* Axel's suits didn't do justice to his athletic build. He was built solid like a tank and his ass looked fabulous. His arms were sculpted and strong. She would have to work hard to keep her eyes off him.

He hadn't seen her enter the lobby. He was on his cell phone with his back to her as she walked up from behind. He must have sensed her presence because he turned around, and then fumbled his cell phone, nearly dropping the thing. He stammered a few parting words on the phone as he ended his call. His eyes stayed glued to her as he feasted on every inch of her body. His lusty gaze made her stomach quiver and knees weak. Not attempting to hide his appraisal or approval, he liked what he saw, and he wanted her to know.

She opened her mouth to speak, the words trapped in Kerrigan's throat, and nothing came out. The rolling waves in her stomach made her queasy like a lovesick teen. She was relieved when he spoke first.

"Hi, Kerrigan. You're timing is perfect. You look …" he paused, his eyes sweeping her up and down again, "… absolutely incredible! You ready?"

"Thank you." Her cheeks warmed. "Yes, I'm ready. Where are we going?"

"We're going to a baseball game. I have a private suite at the stadium. I was just talking to McBride's assistant. He's going to be late. He has some emergency to handle."

"Are you sure he's coming? Maybe we should rain-check?"

"No. We're going regardless." He grabbed her by the hand and pulled her out of the door and toward the parking deck elevator. "Besides, I think you and I could use some fun, with or without McBride. It's only Wednesday, and it's already been a long week. Let's go."

When they reached the elevator, he released her tingling hand, the feeling of his firm grip lingering.

Axel walked her to the passenger side of a black Lexus IS F. His car was luxurious and masculine and sporty. He opened the door and helped her climb inside. The car's interior smelled like him—musky and male, wrecking her senses, and her head spun. He slid into the driver's seat, hit the ignition button, and the car roared to life. They had driven in silence for a few awkward minutes before he broke the tension.

"You like baseball?"

"I'm not a big fan, but going to a live game is always exciting."

"I'm not a big fan either, but the skybox is an investment for entertaining."

"Sounds like a good investment. Do you entertain clients a lot?"

"Yes, mostly. I host office gatherings with the staff and use the space for … recreational outings."

"Recreational outings?" She threw a curious glance at him.

"Yes. Dates."

She frowned. "That's interesting. Do you mean for boy-girl dates? How's that an investment?" She couldn't wait to hear his reasoning. This would be good.

He smiled. "An investment in my future happiness, of course. I don't plan to be a bachelor forever. I'm working hard not to be." She saw him look down at her bare left hand, or perhaps that was in her head. She really had to get a grip.

She was going to set him straight, keep him honest as he had said. "Oh? Sounds as if you're making progress with your lady friend. Have you taken her to one of these games yet?" The thought of him hot and heavy and chasing some random woman made her nauseous.

He ran his left hand through his hair. "I'm making some progress." He rubbed his chin. "She'll be going to a game with me real soon." Cutting his eyes at her, his lips curled up slightly into a faint smirk.

"Good luck. I hope that works out for you." Her stomach knotted.

"I don't need luck. I'm persistent." He glanced at her, and then turned his eyes back to the road.

"Okay. What's the game plan for this evening?" she asked.

The city lights whizzed pass them as they sped down Interstate 75. Glancing in the rear view mirror, he switched lanes, and then exited the highway. "We'll wing this. McBride is a sports buff. I'll engage him on that level. You just be yourself. Charm him with your beauty and brilliant mind. You'll have him eating out of the palm of your hand in no time."

He followed the signs to stadium parking and then parked the car. Insisting that she hold his hand, they weaved through the crowd of fan goers as they made their way up to the skybox. The private suite was much different from what she expected. The room was a good size, but being there alone with Axel made it feel intimate and cramped. Inside was a small dinner table dressed in white linens, a sofa and a minibar.

Kerrigan walked over to the large window that opened to a magnificent view of the field below. Acutely aware of Axel's masculine scent permeating the room and overpowering her senses just like in the car, she patted her heaving chest and sucked in a deep breath. Harris McBride needed to show up soon.

"Kerrigan, please have a seat." He pulled out a chair for her.

She whirled around and made her way to the table, and then he sat beside her.

The loud ring of his cell phone took his attention away from her. This time he answered cryptically, in short clipped phrases while he kept his eyes fixed on her.

He ended the call and shook his head as his fingers danced across the table to the centerpiece, toying with it. "Looks like

McBride can't make the game tonight." She thought she saw a slight smile form at the corner of Axel's mouth.

"Oh? What happened?" Her heart raced, and her mind reeled.

"Didn't get the details. Apparently, his cancellation has something to do with that emergency he's handling. It's a shame. He'll miss a great game." He was glad that McBride cancelled. The sarcastic tone of his voice gave him away.

"So we're staying, even though neither of us likes baseball?" Her voice cracked.

He moved closer to her. "Why not? We don't have to watch the game. We can do other things." His eyes lit up like an amusement park at night. Waving his hands around, he pointed to the room's other amenities, and then stroked his chin. "Like I said before, we can both use a little fun. Kerrigan, are you afraid to have fun with me?"

"No." She paused. "But, what's your idea of fun?"

He put on a big, innocent grin. "We can just hang out. There's food, beer, a TV, music."

It was clear that Axel had every intention of staying and keeping her there with him. Nervous butterflies fluttered inside Kerrigan again—an entire evening in that room alone with Axel would send her over the edge. She didn't know what to do. *He's just a man, and he only wants one thing from you. Just remember that.*

"Are you uncomfortable being alone with me?" he asked.

She leaned back in her chair. "You're the boss. It just feels a little strange *hanging out* with you."

He placed his hand on the table. "You didn't answer my question. Do I make you nervous, Kerrigan?"

She looked down into her lap, fidgeting with her hands. "Yes. You're just so … intense sometimes." *Oh god! Where is he going with this?*

"Hmm. What can we do about that? Any ideas?" he asked as if he enjoyed watching her squirm.

Her eyes narrowed. "You're the boss. We're not friends. I'm under the microscope with you, and that's … well, that's intimidating to me."

He nodded his head. "I see. I don't want you to think of me as the boss. I don't want to intimidate you. Without that title, I'm just like any other man. I have needs, wants, desires, likes and dislikes. Let's just enjoy each other's company and work on becoming friends." He leaped up and headed to the mini bar. "I'll get us some drinks. What would you like?"

Her probing gaze followed him behind the small counter. "I'll take a Coke. Thanks."

He grabbed a beer for himself and a Coke for her and sat them on coasters on the small wooden end table next to the sofa. Taking a seat, he took the remote, turned on the television and began flipping through the channels. "Let's see what's on. Come sit over here with me."

She sat at arms length from him, her posture stiff and movements controlled.

"I promise not to bite unless you want me to," he teased. Sliding closer to her, he cut the divide in half and extended his arm across the back of the sofa.

The hairs at the nape of her neck stood. "No biting." Her strained voice warded off his advance.

Lowering his arm, he cut his eyes at her and slowly nodded his head. "I'll be on my best behavior. I swear," he said.

She shifted in her seat, relaxed her shoulders and leaned back. The tight knot in her stomach loosened. They talked and laughed as they watched an old romantic comedy. Beginning to relax more, she remained cautiously distant. The night was young.

CHAPTER SIX

When the food arrived, they moved back to the table to eat. They made small talk throughout dinner.

"This meal reminds me of my college days. Pizza, burgers, fries. All the great tasting stuff that's off limits to me now" he said, shoving a fry into his mouth. "Hmm. So good."

"I ate stuff like this in high school. By the time I reached college, my palette had matured." She frowned and pushed her plate away.

"Oh come on, don't you eat an occasional French fry?" He teased. Grabbing a fry from the stack on his plate, he taunted her. "Here, open up. At least try one. Here's to trying new things with new friends." His persistence coaxed a bright smile onto her lips.

"Okay. Okay. You win. I'll try one. Once." She bit down, and he fed the fry into her mouth until his fingertips grazed her plump bottom lip. She quickly yanked her head back from his touch. "Umm, that *is* good."

"Only a taste and I have you hooked." The smug tone rolled off his tongue.

"Hooked? Probably not. Fries are the arch nemesis to my hips and thighs."

He pushed against the table, leaned back in his chair and let his eyes roam her body, and then straightened himself to meet her curious expression. "Mmm." He groaned. "Nothing wrong with those thighs or hips. Want more?" Grabbing another fry, he paused one in front of her mouth.

A nervous, breathy laugh escaped her lips. "What are you, a fry dealer?"

He chuckled. "Of sorts."

She closed her eyes and bit into the next one. "Umm, these are great." She chewed behind a guilty smile. Taking his cloth napkin, he dabbed her mouth and then placed the napkin on the table.

He pursed his lips and rubbed his chin. "I enjoy seeing you relaxed, Kerrigan. We're having fun, like a normal…" He paused, carefully considering his next words. "Like normal people getting to know each other." Another pause. "I was never any good at statistics in high school and completely avoided the subject in college, but if I were a betting man, I'd say odds are in my favor that you're getting more comfortable being around me."

"I hated statistics too. What was your favorite subject in high school?" She skirted his calculated statement. Nice move.

He narrowed his eyes, and he reached back into the recesses of his memory. "Let's see. I enjoyed art, English and history best. I had the best English teacher who made words jump off a page into life. What were your favorite subjects?"

Kerrigan stretched her eyes wide; she kept her gaze down, fiddling with a tomato on her plate. "Those were my favorites too." Her voice staggered.

She enticed him, and he couldn't help but to be captivated by her.

"What do you prefer; drama, comedy, action, romance, sci-fi, horror or suspense?" he asked.

"It depends on if you're talking about in my personal life or my movie preference," Kerrigan joked.

He leaned back in his chair again. Pushing both hands through his hair, he gave her a sly grin. "Okay funny lady. Tell me your preference in both." He liked her wit.

She watched him move, and he could tell she liked the way his biceps flexed and bulged. She wasn't immune to him after all. He would use this to his advantage.

"I like it all for movies, but comedy is my number one and then suspense. In my personal life, I'll take romance and action. However, my reality is more like comedy and drama. What about you?" She giggled.

"For movies, I'm a suspense and action guy. My personal life is more like drama and suspense." He leaned forward, softening his tone. "Although, I'd prefer romance and action, too. Something else we have in common."

Their knees touched underneath the table. She shifted away, but he pursued, leaning in closer until his knee found hers again. This time she didn't back away. "Are you having a good time?" he asked.

"Yes, this is really great."

He wanted to touch his salty lips to hers, but the timing wasn't right for a kiss. He needed her to be clear about his intentions before he would make a move as bold as that.

"Good, I'm glad you're having fun. I like hanging out with you. We'll have to do this often—maybe on different terms."

She frowned. "What do you mean on different terms?" She shifted back in her seat away from him.

"I mean on friendlier terms. You're fun, we have lots in common, and I'd like to get to know you better. I think we're becoming friends."

"Um, I don't know if that's a very good idea."

"Why not?"

"Because, you're my boss. I don't want anyone to get the wrong idea."

He wanted to see her squirm again. "Exactly what idea might that be, Kerrigan?"

"Well .... I ... I just think we need professional boundaries. That's all," she stammered.

"The only boundaries are the ones we create. Are you worried that people will think we're more than friends?"

"I don't know what people will think, but I don't need the added drama," she contested.

Axel leaned forward and reached for her hand on the table. "I see. Are you attracted to me, Kerrigan?" He lifted her hand, stroking her fingers with his.

She gasped loudly and pulled her hand away quickly. "I think you're an attractive man," she replied coolly. "But, that doesn't mean ..."

He interrupted her mid-sentence and then stared into her. "Thank you, but that's not what I asked." He repeated the question in a clipped tone. "Are *you* attracted to me, Kerrigan?"

Her eyes glossed over, and she slumped into her seat. He decided to ease up. "You don't have to give me an answer now because you already have, many times. For the record, you should know that I'm a man who doesn't care what others think."

Her eyes flashed with anger. "What others think is important to me, especially since I have to work with them. I'm not interested in being the topic of water-cooler gossip. To answer your extremely direct and unprofessional question, no, there's no attraction."

"You're lying to yourself, Kerrigan."

She pushed away from the table with trembling hands. "Axel, you're dead wrong." The angry shrill of her voice egged him on.

Grabbing her hand, he pulled her back, locking her in place to prevent her escape. "What happened in your office yesterday wasn't very professional, but I felt it, and I know you did too, long before yesterday—there's an unmistakable attraction between us. That doesn't mean we can't be friends. Why deny our chemistry? There's no one here but you and me. Don't you think it's time to deal with the elephant in the room?" Goose bumps trailed along his arms and his stomach churned at the simple touch of holding her hand.

Color rushed to her cheeks. "Axel, I'm sorry, but you're wrong. I'm not attracted to you or interested in you in any way beyond our work relationship." Her lips trembling and eyes shifted.

He smirked. "Fine, if that's how you want to play. We're at least becoming friends, and there's no reason to deny that. When we hang out, we'll be discreet. I don't want us to be the center of office gossip humored as having a steamy office romance."

A sheen of moisture coated her eyes and she turned away. "I'm sorry, Kerrigan. You're upset, and I'm being an ass. Let's work on becoming friends." He hadn't meant to upset her to the point of tears. He would need a new plan to help her face the truth.

After a few seconds of silence, she recovered. Squirming in her chair, she shook her head and rolled her eyes. Glaring at him, she gave him a faint grin. He'd take that over daggers and tears.

"Glad you're seeing things my way. This is an excellent start to a beautiful friendship. You'll see," he teased, trying to lighten the mood.

"I didn't have much choice, did I? You always find a way of getting what you want, don't you?"

He leaned back in his chair deliberately giving her a view of his torso and arms. "Yes, I do. Good you realize this fact early on in our relationship," he said, smiling as he watched her eyes study his frame.

She had no idea of the extent of truth in her words. He always got what he wanted, and he wanted her.

During the ride back to the office, where her car was left, neither spoke. Awkward sideways glances and the occasional sigh was all they exchanged. She wrapped her arms around her body as if shielding herself from the icy vibe that came from him. He didn't want to engage her in conversation. He was sulking at her words. He liked the chase, but he needed to change his strategy if he were going to catch the girl.

He watched her get into her vehicle, and they went their separate ways. He reflected on the events of the evening during his drive home. Twenty minutes later, when he stepped into the kitchen, he found Emma, his housekeeper, making tea. He had confided in her about Kerrigan and respected her advice and views on matters of the heart.

Emma lifted the kettle from the stove and poured steaming hot water into her English teacup. "So…" She paused, turning around from the stove to face him. "How'd your evening go?"

He leaned against the kitchen island, his palms flat on its cold granite surface. He dropped his head in defeat and shrugged his shoulders. "Not exactly like I had hoped." He shook his head. "I frightened Kerrigan and didn't get through to her."

Emma walked around to the side of the island where he stood. "Have you thought about telling her how you feel about her—from your heart?"

He turned to the side to face her. "If I do that, I risk scaring her off for good. I thought spending time together alone would force us to work out our mutual attraction."

The truth was that he was unsure of his feelings.

Emma patted his shoulder gingerly. "You're telling her these meetings are about work, yet you're expecting her to behave unprofessionally. I can understand her hesitation, confusion and even fear."

"Maybe I'm just not her type." He lifted his face to meet a sympathetic smile.

"From everything you've told me about her all these months, I don't think that's the issue. I think you need to try a different approach. After all, you're her boss. Give her time."

Later that night, he retreated to his bedroom. He pulled out his laptop and hammered out an email to her. Reading over the message, he deleted most of the words he had typed. Sharing his feelings in an email was juvenile. He would leave his heart's confession to a time more suitable, where he would have her as his captive audience. Instead, he decided to keep the message short and to the point, and then he hit send.

***

The next morning, Kerrigan's stomach somersaulted at the thought of going to work. The events of the prior evening raced through her head. He was closing in on her, fast, but she was determined not to become another casualty of Axel Christensen. She knew that while he found her attractive, he was probably exploring some fetish or fantasy. Maybe he wanted to know what it would be like with a woman different from his usual type or to have an office affair. Perhaps he wondered what sex would be like with a black woman, but she wasn't going to be his lab rat.

She walked into her office, sat down at her desk and logged on to her computer. She had already received several emails in her in-box, but one stood out from all the others. It was from Axel's personal email address.

12:03 a.m. on Thursday, August 23

To: Kerrigan Mulls

From: Axel Christensen

Subject: Last Night

Kerrigan,

I had a terrific time with you last night. I'm glad we reached an understanding about our friendship. I hope you enjoyed yourself. I'd love you to join me for lunch tomorrow. I'll stop by your office at noon. I also have tickets to a play that I hear is fabulous. It's next Saturday evening at 6:00 p.m. It's not with McBride. It's just you and me going out for dinner and a play. I can pick you up at your place at 5:00 p.m. I'm eager to spend time with you.

Your friend,

Axel

A shiver ran down her spine. She was flattered, but he was moving too fast and that frightened her. She really liked him, but his reputation preceded him. She would be wise to remember that. Thinking carefully about her reply, she responded.

8:35 a.m. on Thursday, August 23

To: Axel Christensen

From: Kerrigan Mulls

Subject: Next Saturday

Axel,

I enjoyed myself at the game. I am free for lunch on Friday. I assume you want to discuss my presentation. Next Saturday sounds like fun, but I have a date that evening. Maybe some other time.

Your friend,

Kerrigan

She didn't have a date. In fact, she positively had nothing to do, but she needed an excuse to keep him at bay. Kerrigan was inflamed and enthralled with him, and her feelings scared the hell out of her. If she allowed him to get too close, she wouldn't be able to resist him.

He fired a response back immediately, this time much more direct.

8:47 a.m. on Thursday, August 23

To: Kerrigan Mulls

From: Axel Christensen

Subject: Change Your Plans

Kerrigan,

Change your plans next Saturday. I have to see you to discuss an important matter. I'll pick you up at 5:00 p.m.

Your friend,

Axel

She couldn't believe his gall, yet she was intrigued and amused, and his commanding tone excited her. She wanted to know what could be so urgent that he *had* to see her next Saturday.

8:50 a.m. on Thursday, August 23

To: Axel Christensen

From: Kerrigan Mulls

Subject: Change My Plans

Axel,

I'll see what I can do. Are you always this demanding with your friends?

Kerrigan

His reply was brief but direct. Didn't he have work to do or a meeting to attend?

8:52 a.m. on Thursday, August 23

To: Kerrigan Mulls

From Axel Christensen

Subject: Regarding your question

Yes, especially where you're concerned. I'll see you tomorrow at lunch.

Your friend,

Axel

The rest of the day was a drag. She went from one meeting to another, feeling as though she hadn't accomplished anything all day. At four thirty, Ashley walked in and shut the door.

"Kerri, so what's new? Something you care to tell me?" An accusation peppered her escalating tone.

Kerrigan frowned, and her eyes darted from one corner of the room to the other. "Nothing in particular. What am I supposed to tell you?"

Ashley slid into one of her empty guest chairs and the sides of her lips contracted into a pucker. "Only that you had a date with Axel last night!" Her excited, high-pitched squeal pierced Kerrigan's ears.

"What? What on earth are you talking about?"

"Sue from accounting said she saw you and Axel leave the office together last night. She was in the garage and saw you get into his car. You're holding out on me."

She huffed and grabbed the nape of neck, her eyes slit into a squint. "Axel and I were supposed to entertain McBride last night. We went to a baseball game, but McBride had some emergency and canceled at the last minute." The thought of Sue telling everyone in the office what she had seen made Kerrigan's insides roll. "That old bat makes me sick."

Ashley raised her eyebrows at her friend. "Uh huh, and you believe McBride had to cancel? Did you talk to him or his people yourself?"

Her elbows planted on the desk, Kerrigan rested the weight of her head in her hands and scrunched her face. "Yes, I believe McBride canceled. Why would Axel make up a thing like that?"

"Duh! He wants to spend time alone with you. That, my friend, was a date."

She thought over Ashley's accusation. She remembered the phone calls. There couldn't be any truth to Ashley's words. "I don't think that's what happened. I heard him take the phone calls from McBride's people. I truly believe McBride had an emergency." She folded her arms across her chest, taking a defensive posture.

"I'm just saying, the excuse sure sounds awful convenient. So, how did the date that wasn't supposed to be a date go?"

She shrugged her shoulders and sighed. "Uh … interesting. We talked a lot—found out we have a lot in common."

Ashley shifted in her seat, eager to hear more. "Uh huh. What else? Did he make a move?"

"Sort of, I guess." She coiled her arms around her body, bracing for Ashley's reaction.

"What! What happened?" Ashley nearly came out of her chair with excitement.

"He confronted me about our attraction, asked me if I was attracted to him." She remembered how nervous she had been.

Ashley's eyes grew wide and wild. "He did?" She gasped, and her jaw dropped. "Oh my god! What did you say?"

"I denied his accusation, of course. I told him there was no attraction."

"You said that? Then what did he say?"

"He doesn't believe me, but said we should be friends." She omitted the intense sexual interlude that had occurred between them in her office.

Ashley tilted her head. "Axel Christensen is many things, but among them is not BFF to a sexy little number like you. He's in full pursuit. Just be careful. A man like him isn't satisfied until he gets what he wants, and men like that usually get what they want. You need to find out what that is."

Kerrigan placed her hands on the desk, fiddling with a pen. "I know exactly what he wants. I just hope my willpower outlasts his."

"That's what he's counting on—that he'll wear you down. I just don't want to see you get hurt. If you decide you want to have a little fun, then fine, but I see the way you look at him. Kerri, I'm your friend, and I can see that you really like him." Ashley shook her head. "I should warn you that Sue is telling people what she saw. She's a terrible gossip. I know you're a big girl. Just be careful. Please."

She didn't deny anything Ashley said because she was right. She had never felt like this about a man.

She nodded and gave Ashley a serious look. "Thanks, Ash. I will."

CHAPTER SEVEN

Friday, August 24

It was a quarter to noon on Friday. Axel was making his way to Kerrigan's office for lunch when he saw Sue McCleary standing near her office. He knew Sue was a troublemaker. He also remembered what Kerrigan said about not wanting to be the topic of office conversation in the break room. He wanted to keep her safe, even from silly office rumors. He continued pass Kerrigan's office, went to the break room and pulled out his phone.

"Hello. A.C. Advertising. This is Kerrigan Mulls."

"Hi, Kerrigan."

Her rapid words and pitched voice unveiled her excitement. "Axel? Hi."

The sound of her voice warmed him like flames blazing from a July sun. "Hi. You ready for lunch?"

"Sure."

"Can we meet someplace else? I'm trying to respect your concern for privacy and discretion. I don't want to start any rumors about us."

"Too late for that. Rumors are already flying."

"Rumors are flying about what?" His voice was tense.

"Sue saw us leaving together on Wednesday night. I don't know what lies she's spreading, but I've been getting strange looks all morning."

Axel wasn't annoyed or bothered by office gossip, but he knew Kerrigan was upset and instant rage elevated his pulse.

He paced the floor in the break room. "I'm sorry. I can only imagine how you must be feeling. You okay?"

"Yes, I'm fine. I've been ignoring them."

"I still want to see you. Can you meet me some place? What about Tedd's?"

He didn't attempt to mask the hungry desperation in his voice. It was soulful longing, something he knew she would recognize, because although she wouldn't admit her feelings to him, he knew she felt the same as he did.

"All right, I'll leave now." She paused. "Axel, thank you for understanding."

"Of course. I don't want you upset."

He was already seated when Kerrigan strolled in and found him at the rear of the restaurant. Lunch with her was fun. He always enjoyed the time they spent together, and she seemed to enjoy his company too, although she kept her guard up.

She picked up her fork and poked at her salad. "Exactly why do I need to cancel my plans next Saturday? What's going on?" she asked.

He thought for a minute before responding. In that instant, he could have lain out his heart and told her how he had been feeling and how much he liked her. How for months, he watched and yearned to be close to her—how much more he liked her now that he was getting to know her better—how much he admired her intelligence and delighted in her beauty. Instead...

"I'll be out of town all next week for business. I leave this Sunday, and I get back late Friday evening. We'll need to catch up immediately."

"Oh? And we can't catch up the following week?" she asked.

He shook his head. "No. I'm not available that week until Friday."

Clearing her throat, she brought the glass of water to her lips and sipped. "So this is related to business?"

He leaned in close, glancing around at the restaurant's patrons as his eyes steadied and met hers. "Yes. Well, no." Everything around them faded away, including baldy, a businessman who was sitting alone at the next table eavesdropping and ogling at Kerrigan.

Her glass dropped to the clothed table with a loud thud, and she swallowed hard. Kerrigan's eyes shifted around the room. A waiter, whose mullet was straight out of a 1980's rock video, stood at the back of the restaurant gawking at them. Kerrigan jerked her hand away and sent the glass into a teeter. Axel's quick aim landed his hand on hers, and their entwined fingers held the glass steady. Her fingers struggled to break away from the slick, wet cylinder, but his firm grasp held her hand in place. Slowly, she lifted wide nervous eyes to his, and he released her hand.

"Kerrigan, I'd be lying if I said there wasn't a personal angle. I enjoy spending time with you. You're good company, and we have fun together. Isn't that what friends do?" The desperation in his voice spoke loudly.

"You're going to miss me." She teased boldly.

The dim light from the pendant hanging overhead danced off her angelic face and highlighted the brown and golden tones in Kerrigan's wavy hair that flowed over her shoulder, gently caressing her right cheek.

His pulse quickened. "Yes, I'm going to miss you, very much." Her darting eyes stilled, fixed to his, and she froze. "And I know you're going to miss me too." A hard lump formed in his throat and his chest tightened, waiting for her reply.

He held her gaze. Beauty radiated from her frigid face. Melting the ice, the corners of her mouth curled into a warm smile. "Then I suppose I can make an exception just this once. May I ask about your trip? Where are you going?"

Tense shoulders relaxing, he swallowed hard and then exhaled. "Yes, of course. I'm going to meet some clients in Denver. They want to discuss a new national campaign for their ski resort." Wiping his mouth with his napkin as he glanced around, the background came into view again. "I thought I'd invite you along, but I know the kind of rumors that would stir."

"I think you're right about the rumors. I wouldn't have gone anyway," she said.

If she had gone with him, he would have made sure that the rumors held merit.

When lunch ended, they walked to the restaurant's waiting area. He guided them to a private corner, surrounded by greenery, to finish their conversation.

Standing close, "While I'm gone, can you gather research on McBride's markets?" he asked softly.

"Sure. I'll have the data ready in time for our next meeting."

"Great. Thank you." He paused and glimpsed around, discovering they were isolated. "I think we should say our goodbyes here. I know how nervous you are about rumors."

She extended her arm for a handshake.

Forehead wrinkling, a glint of a smile crossed his lips. He stepped forward, no more than an inch between them. She didn't move. "I think we can do better than that," he said.

Intensely focused on nothing but her, for a brief moment, he and Kerrigan were the only two people in the room. With a quick motion, he wrapped his arms around her tiny waist, pulled her close to him until her tender breasts pressed into his chest. Kerrigan's small hands landed on his biceps, her fingers digging into his arms through his shirtsleeves.

"What are you doing?" She whispered into his chest, her head hung down forestalling his gaze.

"Saying goodbye." Leaning down, he nuzzled his head in the crook of her neck, inhaling the sweet fragrance that was uniquely hers. "Umm." He released a low guttural groan and closed his eyes, succumbing to the serenity that settled over him with her nestled in his arms. Her head tilted to the side, giving him greater access. Softly, his lips brushed the throbbing vein in her neck.

A small gasp escaped her.

The tightening in his chest and knot in his stomach dissipated, replaced by boiling blood rushing through his system and sending him into a stupor. Like rock forming from molten lava, his desire rose, and his erection pressed into her. Trembling hands pushed hard against him, but he tightened his grip and held her in place, ending her protest. Slowly, tenderly and with skilled precision, he planted soft feather light kisses up her neck, along her jaw line to her cheek and then his lips touched the corner of her mouth.

"Uh, um." The loud sound of a man clearing his throat jostled him out of his fog, and he stopped abruptly. His hands dropped from her waist, and he stepped back. Glancing around, he met the stark stare of two nearby patrons. The haggard cock blocker had the audacity to wink. He had never wanted to kiss her more than he did in that moment. Again, the kiss would have to wait. Although he didn't intend for their hug to be platonic, he never expected to get lost in her. His head reeling and heart racing, the only thing on his mind was Kerrigan. The hug was a lover's embrace, a promise of things to come. Mission accomplished.

***

Kerrigan zipped through crowds of business people along the sidewalk as she hurried back to the office on shaky legs, her head spinning and her heart hammered in her chest. She mulled over the hug-almost-kiss or whatever had just happened. Remembering the feeling of Axel's body pressed against hers, his hands caressing the small of her back and his hot breath and soft kisses on her neck made her knees buckle. Nearly going down right there on the sideway, she spotted her rescue a few feet ahead. She made a frantic dash and threw her arms around the lamppost to steady and keep her upright. Opened-mouth stares and quizzical frowns of passersby greeted her.

"Miss, are you all right?" A woman's small hand touched her shoulder.

Closing her eyes, she threw her head back and let out a small laugh. "Yes, I need my head examined, but I'm fine. Thank you."

***

The door slammed. She rushed over to the desk and tossed herself into the seat. Her reaction was ridiculous. If he had succeeded in his attempt to kiss her, she would have burst into flames right there on the spot. Groaning loudly, she buried her head in her folded arms on the desk. Axel being away for a week was good. Distance was good—just the reprieve needed to calm her raging hormones and regain her senses, yet she was too far-gone now having tasted his appetite for her. The minutes ticked away slowly as the afternoon dragged along. Knowing she wouldn't see him next week, she slumped over her desk lacking any motivation to work, her mind distracted by a whirling sea of emotions churning her belly and thoughts flooding her mind.

The sound of an incoming email snatched her from her musing. A personal email from Axel appeared in her in-box.

4:43 p.m. on Friday, August 24

To: Kerrigan Mulls

From: Axel Christensen

Subject: Next Week

Hi Kerrigan,

As always, I enjoyed your company at lunch today, especially the end. I'll have to go away often. Check your email while I'm gone.

...to be continued.

Your friend,

Axel

P.S. – Don't go out on any dates this weekend.

A sharp pang struck her chest. He was a flirt, but his words and actions held something more promising. At least she wanted to believe that. She decided not to write back. She would wait for another email from him. As the day dragged on, she couldn't wait, for the weekend to start. There had been strange stares and hushed conversations happening throughout the office. She tried to ignore them, but they still bothered her. Finally, at six o'clock her day ended. She packed her things and headed home. Axel would be missed.

CHAPTER EIGHT

The weekend whirled pass, and the week crawled along slowly. The first email Kerrigan received from Axel came Saturday morning.

9:02 a.m. on Saturday, August 25
To: Kerrigan Mulls
From: Axel Christensen
Subject: Hello from Denver
Hi Kerrigan,
I arrived in Denver safely. It's lovely here. I'm going to meet with the owners today, and then I'm heading to tour and go sightseeing. Wish you could be here with me to see this place. It's magnificent.
Your Friend,
Axel

***

11:00 a.m. on Saturday, August 25
To: Axel Christensen
From: Kerrigan Mulls
Subject: Re: Hello from Denver
Hi Axel,

I'm glad your flight went well. I hope your meeting goes well too. Take some pictures on your tour. I'd like to see them.
Your Friend,
Kerrigan

***

7:34 a.m. on Sunday, August 26
To: Kerrigan Mulls
From: Axel Christensen
Subject: At your request
Hey Kerrigan,
The tour was excellent. I've been here before, but never had a chance to enjoy the place. I'm in love with Denver. I'll have to come back, but next time I'll bring you with me. I've attached some photos. You'll notice me in some them. I'm the lonely guy who wishes his friend was here too.
Your Friend,
Axel

***

9:16 a.m. on Sunday, August 26
To: Axel Christensen
From: Kerrigan Mulls
Subject: Lonely in Denver
Axel,
Thanks for sharing those pictures with me! Although Denver looks lovely, I can't think of any reason why you and I would need to go together. Sorry you're lonely. Denver is crawling with people. I'm sure you'll meet another new friend in no time.
Your Friend,
Kerrigan

***

5:36 p.m. on Sunday, August 26
To: Kerrigan Mulls
From: Axel Christensen
Subject: Re: Lonely in Denver
Kerrigan,
Glad you liked the pictures. I can think of a few reasons for you to be here with me. Should I elaborate or would you like to use your imagination? I'm not interested in meeting new friends in Denver. I'm very selective about the company I keep. Besides, my new friend in Atlanta is all I want. I'm especially exclusive as far as our friendship is concerned.
Your Friend,
Axel

***

9:24 a.m. on Monday, August 27
To: Axel Christensen
From: Kerrigan Mulls
Subject: Speaking of friends
Axel,
There's no need to elaborate. I think you've made yourself quite clear, which is exactly why I'm never going to Denver with you. Being selective is good. Speaking of exclusive friendships, how is the lady friend you told me about? You know, the one you planned to take on a date to your private suite at the stadium. The same one you said is worth the wait. Sure sounds like you're trying to live up to your tabloid reputation.
Your Friend,
Kerrigan

***

10:46 p.m. on Monday, August 27
To: Kerrigan Mulls
From: Axel Christensen
Subject: Re: *Speaking of friends*
Kerrigan,
Never say never. Mark my words, you will come to Denver with me one day. If I didn't know better, I would say there was a hint of jealously in your last email. There's no need for that. I told you, I'm not a bachelor by choice. I'm working hard to change my eligibility status with my lady friend. I did take her out on a date. In fact, we reached an agreement to become friends. I had a terrific time. I thought she enjoyed herself too. You did say you had a good time at the game, didn't you Kerrigan?
Patiently waiting in Denver,
Axel

She read his last email over, and over again. He had left her no doubt that he was interested in her and confirmed that she was the mystery woman that he had been talking about. Seized by some unrecognizable emotion, her stomach rolled. Axel was making a full-on play for her affection.

By Tuesday afternoon, she still hadn't responded to his direct email. She wasn't sure what to say exactly. Finally, mustering courage enough to reply, she typed, but as she did, another email from him came in.

4:53 p.m. on Tuesday, August 28
To: Kerrigan Mulls
From: Axel Christensen
Subject: Scared?
Hey Kerrigan,
Did I scare you off? If you don't respond in the next ten minutes, I'll call you.

Not-so-patiently waiting in Denver,
Axel

***

4:55 p.m. on Tuesday, August 28
To: Axel Christensen
From: Kerrigan Mulls
Subject: Yes
Axel,
Please don't call. I've told you that I'm not interested in you beyond our work relationship and at most, friendship. Can we talk on Saturday?
Kerrigan

***

Kerrigan didn't hear back from Axel. Despite the herbal teas and antacid tablets she took, the nausea in her belly wouldn't go away. He was known for his short fuse, hot temper and impatience. The 'can we talk' line was the kiss of death, but she hadn't meant it quite that way. Had her last email inspired him to take her advice and try out Denver's local flavor of women? She pushed the thoughts away and tried to focus on her work. Regardless of whatever was happening between them, she needed to stay focused on the McBride account. She couldn't run away from her job.

On Wednesday evening, she received a message from his work email address. It was direct, demanding and short, void of anything seemingly personal.

11:53 p.m. on Wednesday, August 29
To: Kerrigan Mulls
From: Axel Christensen
Subject: Coming back early

Kerrigan,

Change of plans. I'll be back in the office on Friday. We need to meet. Brenda will send follow-up details. We're off for Saturday.

Axel Christensen

President and Chief Executive Officer

A.C. Advertising

A wave of nausea flooded over her, and she flinched. She wasn't sure what his email meant, but she noted the change in his signature. Her eyes welled up with tears at the thought that he had given up on her. She had made it impossible for him to think there could be anything more than a friendly work relationship between them. That's what she had been working so hard to accomplish. Her tears flowed freely as she drifted into a restless sleep, the painful sting of regret chasing her into unconsciousness.

CHAPTER NINE

Friday, August 31

Axel sat at his desk staring at his computer screen eagerly awaiting Kerrigan's arrival. He had asked Brenda to leave a message for her that morning, explaining that he needed to see her right away. He glanced at the time—a few minutes after nine o'clock. He knew she was probably in the office by then. Minutes later, he heard a light tap at the door. He took a deep breath and exhaled.

"Come in." The thunder of his deep bravado reverberated off the walls.

Just thinking about Kerrigan heightened his anxiety. The sight of her always made his palms dampen and his throat dry. He couldn't wait to see her again, to talk to her, to be near her, to smell her sweet scent. The large doors opened slowly, and his gut wrenched.

Axel jumped up from his seat. His jaw dropped. "What, what in the hell are you doing in my office?"

"Well, hello to you too."

Misty strolled over to his desk, her large leather handbag smacking against her side. A boney hand rested on her right hip and she rolled her eyes. "Oh, come on, Axel. I remember a time when you were always glad to see me. I was in the neighborhood and thought I'd stop by to say hello."

His eyes swept her tall, thin form. "Misty, I don't know why you're here. How did you get pass Brenda?"

Misty peeled her jacket away and tossed the garment on the red leather sofa. "Brenda wasn't at her desk." Her cherry red heels tapped against the floor as she strutted around his desk and paused in front of him. "My timing couldn't have been better. Don't you agree?" Misty spun around, her bare-naked ass and breasts were within inches of Axel's twitching fingers.

Axel's eyes stretched wide. He swallowed hard. "Misty, put your goddamn clothes on. Now!" His loud yell didn't rattle her.

Taking large steps to put distance between them, he moved to the other side of the desk.

Misty followed. She sank her nails into Axel's biceps, forced herself onto him. "Axel, you know you want this. What's stopping you?" She batted her green eyes and smiled.

He jerked away and took two steps back. "Misty, I've already told you. You and I are done. I, I'm involved with someone else." Losing his footing, Axel stumbled and plunged onto the sofa, bringing Misty's naked body flush on top of his.

The doors to Axel's office opened slowly. "Ah!" The loud gasp commanded his attention.

Kerrigan's eyes filled with tears. Her jaw trembled. Cupping her mouth as she gasped for air, she turned, and then fled.

Axel shoved Misty aside, sending her tumbling to the cold hardwood floor. He stood and ran to the doorway. His heart hammered and his clammy hands forced the doors open. "Kerrigan, wait. Please. Kerrigan, this isn't what you think. Wait, please." She was gone.

***

"I can't believe I'm about to say this, but…" Ashley paused, adjusted herself in the seat. "Maybe Misty threw herself at Axel."

Her lips trembled. "Ash, I don't care. He can do whatever, whenever, with whomever he pleases. What I saw proved exactly what I already know to be true. Axel Christensen can't be trusted." Kerrigan whispered and waived her hand, a dismissive gesture. She didn't want the people sitting at the other end of the long table to hear their conversation.

"How long are you going to ignore the man? He's still your boss." Ashley glanced at the conference room door. The door handle jingled.

"He may be my boss, but that doesn't entitle him to treat me however he pleases." Kerrigan glanced up as Megan and Rich walked in. She cut a sideways glance at Ashley. "I'm done talking about this."

Rich took the seat directly next to Kerrigan. Megan plopped down across from Ashley.

He cut his eyes at Kerrigan and then passed a furtive glance to Megan. "Kerrigan, are you giving an update on the Hollister account?" Rich asked, a smug grin possessing his thin lips.

"Yes, I am."

"Hmm. That'll be a short update," he grumbled under his breath.

Megan laughed. "Four people managed that account before you did, Kerrigan. I can't imagine that you could make much more progress than any one of them."

"That's where you'd be wrong, Megan." A hush fell across the room at the sound of the deep baritone voice.

Axel stood at the head of the table, his scowl directed at Rich, and then Megan.

Megan cleared her throat and wrestled in her chair. "Oh, Mr. Christensen. I, I didn't see you come in; didn't realize you'd be joining us today."

"Obviously," he scolded as he took his seat. "Kerrigan, can you give the team an update? We're all interested in your progress, including me, since you've canceled our last four one-on-one meetings."

Girding herself against Axel's intense stare and icy tone, she stood and walked to the projector screen, directly behind him.

Axel wheeled his chair to the side and extended his arm. "Here, take the pointer."

Kerrigan reached for the device. Their eyes met in a fleeting glance and the tips of his fingers grazed hers, sent scorching heat up her arm. She pivoted on her heel. Her back facing the audience, she swallowed hard. She hated how he affected her, made her knees wobble and stomach quiver.

Regaining her center, she straightened her shoulders and looked pass Axel, her focus on the other faces in the room. "I've been hard at work with the Hollister team for the past few weeks. I had to rebuild their trust. The good news is that I convinced the head of their marketing department to give A.C. Advertising one more chance."

Catching Axel's narrow gaze unnerved her and the pointer slipped out of her sweaty palms. Kerrigan squatted to retrieve contraption that had landed next to his chair. The unexpected heat of Axel's hand on hers as he kneeled beside her forced her eyes to his.

He mouthed silently, "We need to talk."

"Fine," she whispered, and then stood.

Kerrigan advanced the slides. "Hollister owns less than five percent of the market today. Here are income projections over the next ten years for Hollister's main customer base—doctors, lawyers, executives." Her eyes landed on Axel, who stared back, rubbing his chin. "The options I outlined for Hollister were very simple. Get serious about their marketing efforts now or go out of business within three years." Kerrigan glanced at Megan, and then at Rich. "The challenge they have is building and holding onto a loyal customer base. Hollister needs a loyalty program targeted to their most distinguished clients who have the discretionary income to spend at their retail stores. They have to make those customers feel like they belong to an exclusive group." Kerrigan advanced the slides again. "I delivered three concepts around a strategy that I'm calling Platinum Rewards that encourages and rewards loyalty. Early this week, I received the call. They signed a three and half million dollar contract with us."

Megan's mouth dropped open. Rich squirmed in his seat, ogling Kerrigan.

"This morning, I received a call from the head of marketing at Hollister." Axel glanced around the room and halted his gaze on Kerrigan. "She said Kerrigan presented a compelling case. I'm sure you'll become an expert on the meaning of loyalty." Kerrigan flustered at his scalding stare and the inflection of his voice. "Outstanding work," Axel said flatly.

"Thank you." Kerrigan took her seat at the table.

The meeting continued and the account managers went around the table sharing client updates. Axel remained quiet, but kept his eyes on Kerrigan until the end.

"Everyone, let's get back to work," he said dismissing the team. "Kerrigan, I need to speak with you now."

The room cleared out and Kerrigan didn't budge from her spot at the table.

Axel strolled to the window behind her, placed his hands in his pockets. His musky scent made her lightheaded.

"Kerrigan, I commend you for your work. I've always believed in your talent, supported your decisions." He whirled around and leaned against the table, directly facing her. "Imagine my surprise when Diane at Hollister told me that she had interviewed you for a junior-level research position at her company." She peered up at him blinking rapidly. "Hmm. Loyalty," he muttered under his breath.

Her belly fluttered as the intensity between them grew. "Diane approached me. The position isn't in sales and I'm not in violation of the non-compete disclosure. I, I…"

He leaned down, his frowning mug inches from her glistening brow. "I don't care about that damned disclosure, Kerrigan. This is what you want? Career suicide. Simply to get away from me." He stood, and paced from the door to the table where she remained seated. "Kerrigan, Misty Scott doesn't mean anything to me. She came to my office, stripped her clothes off and threw herself at me." His eyes narrowed on her. "Do whatever you want. I just wanted you to know the truth in case that incident had any bearing on your decision to leave." His large hand covered the doorknob. "I want you … here at A.C. Advertising." His eyes flashed with tenderness quickly replaced by a frigid glare. "Whatever you decide, I want to hear from you directly, not from Marie, not from Diane. If you leave me, Kerrigan, I expect for you to tell me face-to-face."

The knob twisted and he shut the door behind him. Left in the room alone, Kerrigan buried her face in her palms. If he was telling the truth about Misty, she would be making the biggest mistake in her life.

***

Saturday, September 15

For weeks, Kerrigan had managed to do everything in her power to avoid Axel, but she hadn't found a way to forget him. Even now, lounging on the sandy shore under an umbrella with a book in one hand and a drink in the other hand, she couldn't stop thinking about the man. The last minute decision to take a mini vacation on Tybee Island wasn't the most thought out plan she'd ever made, but she needed a break. She needed time to make her decision.

"Kerri, snap out of it. Everything is going to be fine." Ashley's gentle hand caressed Kerrigan's forearm rested on the lounge chair's edge.

Kerrigan shook her head. "I know. I'm just nervous about telling him."

Ashley tilted her head, gazing at her friend through expensive designer sun glasses as she relaxed on the lounger next to Kerrigan. "You don't owe Axel Christensen anything. He doesn't own you. If you want to leave the company, then accept the position at Hollister. But, Kerri, if you're taking that job to run away from Axel or your feelings, then you'll be disappointed in yourself. Are you sure this is what you really want?"

Kerrigan shot up in her seat. "Ash, I know this doesn't make sense to you, but I have to get away from him. After seeing him with that naked woman in his office and thinking about what would have happened if I hadn't walked in …" Her stomach rolled in waves. "Leaving A.C. Advertising is the best thing for me."

"I hear you, Kerri, but Axel knew you were coming to his office. In fact, he arranged those meetings so that he could get closer to you. He's been chasing you since day one. The thing with Misty just doesn't add up."

"Ash, the man is a player. Nothing has to add up. The opportunity was there and well," she said glancing at an incoming call. "I can't believe this. I've spoken the devil up." She lifted the cellphone to Ashley, showing her Axel's phone number flashing on the screen.

Ashley leaped forward and snatched the phone from Kerrigan's slippery hands.

Kerrigan lunged forward, tumbling to the sand. "Ash, don't you dare answer that call."

A playful grin emerged, Ashley pressed the speaker button. "Hello," Ashley said.

Throwing a tantrum, Kerrigan waved her arms in protest, and then tossed a handful of sand at Ashley. "Hi, Kerrigan?" The sound of Axel's voice made Kerrigan's throat dry and she couldn't speak.

"Kerrigan, its Axel. Hello?"

Kerrigan pressed her lips together tightly, refusing to speak.

"Oh, hi there. This is Ashley. Kerri, uh, Kerrigan can't come to the phone right now. I'll tell her you called." She took Axel off of the speaker and jerked away from Kerrigan's clawed hands.

"Thank you, Ashley. Tell her to check her email."

"Um, okay." Ashley stared at Kerrigan. "I'll tell her to check her email."

Kerrigan rolled her eyes at Ashley.

"Let her know that I called about the Hollister situation."

Ashley nodded her head. "Yes sir, I'll let her know you want to talk about the Hollister situation."

"And Ashley, we both know that Kerrigan is sitting there next to you, which is why you're repeating everything I'm saying. Tell her I will call back in five minutes and she'd better answer."

Ashley's eyes widened. "Yes, I'll make sure she gets the message."

Ending the call, Ashley handed the phone to Kerrigan, and then stood. "Yeah, I'm going down to the water. Oh, and Axel will be calling you in five minutes. He expects you to answer." Adjusting her bikini top, she strutted toward the water's edge.

"Ugh! I can't believe him." Kerrigan yelled out.

"Just take the damn call," Ashley yelled back.

The phone buzzed again. Kerrigan's small fingers glided to the talk button. "Hello, Axel."

"Hi." The mere sound of his voice raised her temperature.

Reclining in her seat again, she griped the phone tightly. "I'm on vacation. Do you need something?"

"Yes. I need you to believe me. Misty was the aggressor. I've been completely honest with you. What can I do to convince you to stay?"

"Axel, as long as I'm at A.C. Advertising, you're my boss. We can't blur the lines, we can't be..."

"Anything more than friends," he finished her sentence.

"Exactly."

"Kerrigan, do really want to work for Hollister doing research?"

She let out a sigh. "I haven't made my decision."

"We need to meet and you need to give me an answer. When are you back?"

She gazed down at the shore. Ashley was flirting with a tall muscular man wearing a bright yellow speedo. She shook her head at her friend. "I'll be back next week."

"Good. Brenda will set up a time for us to talk."

"Fine."

Axel chuckled softly. "I'm curious. If you're not interested in anything more than friendship, why did seeing me with Misty make you so upset?"

Kerrigan took a swig of her drink. Her palms moistened. "I, I think anyone would be upset to walk into their boss's office and find him romping around with his naked girlfriend." Her stomach quivered. She hoped he would believe her explanation.

"Misty Scott is not my girlfriend and I wasn't romping around with her. I need you to believe me."

"Fine. Suppose I believe you. What difference does that make?"

He laughed. "Your trust in me makes all the difference in the world. Enjoy your vacation, Kerrigan. I'll see you when you get back."

She checked the phone's screen. Their call was properly disconnected. "Ugh," the exasperated sound escaped her lungs. Kerrigan rested her head against the lounger and closed her eyes. The sun's rays searing her flesh mimicked the affect Axel had on her.

"Get out of my head," She yelled out. "What's wrong with me?"

Her fingers slid across the phone's screen, a text message typed to Axel in defeat:

I'm not interested in anything more than friendship.

His instantaneous response enraged her:

Glad you're staying. See you soon, friend. ☺

He hadn't said anything out of place and he hadn't gloated, but she imagined the smug grin he must have worn.

She replied, firing back on defensive impulse:

I didn't say I was staying.

His next message received an hour later seemed void of emotion.

Meeting in my office, Friday at 9 a.m.

Her stomach clenched. She wondered why the sudden change in the tone of his text.

What are we meeting about?

This time, there was no response from Axel.

CHAPTER TEN

Friday, September 21

For the first time in weeks, Axel and Kerrigan would meet. On the agenda was an urgent matter related to the McBride account. Their last botched effort to meet with Harris McBride was a month ago.

There she stood, radiant with hesitation riddled across her face. Taking small, measured steps, she nervously entered and her eyes darted across the room, never making direct contact with his. Once inside, she stood motionless, unsure of herself and scared, as though she didn't know what to do next.

"Close the doors, Kerrigan and have a seat at the table," he said in a commanding tone, exerting his control over the situation.

Behind his desk at the other end of the room, he sat stone-faced, eyes tracing her delicate form as she floated across the floor to the conference table. Standing, he casually strode to the table and plopped into a chair near Kerrigan, sitting as close as possible. Axel knew exactly what he was doing to her. After all, she deserved the torment. While she had been scared off by his directness, he didn't like how she had handled the situation. She wanted him just as badly as he wanted her, and he would give her the jolt she needed. Remaining quiet, he didn't speak with words. Instead, he let his expression communicate his thoughts. His eyes raked her over as he clenched his jaw and pinned her with his glassy stare.

"Hi. I saw the meeting invitation. Why are we meeting tonight?" Kerrigan asked softly, her voice barely above a whisper while she avoided his brooding gaze with her eyes fixed on restless hands tumbling in her lap.

He wasn't sure how she felt about seeing him after his snappy text message, but he wasn't in a mood to be challenged.

He continued glaring at her. "Tonight is about you and me, Kerrigan. We need to talk about how we'll continue working together."

Flicking her eyes upward, she rolled them and huffed.

"Not interested? Am I keeping you from a hot date this evening?" She opened her mouth to speak, but he cut her off before she could utter a response. "As the account manager, I assumed you were the right person for the job, and I expect loyalty. I need someone dependable in this position. Have you decided to take the research position at Hollister? Should I look for your replacement?" This was a move of desperation on his part, but he wasn't afraid to call her bluff.

She took a deep breath and exhaled, jostled by his harsh tone. "Um, no. I didn't take the position at Hollister. You can depend on me. Tonight will be fine," she replied almost inaudibly.

Relieved that she was staying at his company, the heaviness in his chest lifted. His excitement masked, he pressed on. "Kerrigan, I'm glad you're staying, but don't want to interrupt your personal life. If you have other plans this evening, we can meet next week. It's your call."

He studied her intensely. He had missed her beautiful face, now hollow and drawn with dampened eyes.

She batted her eyes fighting tears. "I'm free this evening, and no, I don't have any personal plans. I know how critical it is for us to work together."

"Good, then we're set for seven-thirty. That's all. I'll see you this evening." He wasn't satisfied with her answer. She didn't address her dating status, but he decided not to badger her.

The meeting was done, and Kerrigan gathered her things. She stood, and he watched her without saying a word. She moved so gracefully. He wanted to hold her rounded hips in his hands, to taste her plump lips, to savor her scent. Just as determined, he wanted to claim her heart, mind, body and soul. Growing hard, his cock jumped to life. He would have to wait a few minutes before getting up to keep his bulge concealed.

She paused before walking away from the table where they sat. "Goodbye, Axel."

He tilted his head and smiled coyly, offering a parting comment to dismiss her. "We'll be working very closely together, Kerrigan. Although you've wounded my pride, I know how to remain professional. I have another meeting. See you tonight."

She nodded her head and sprinted for the door, making her retreat.

***

Axel was deep in thought when Rob waltzed into his office, trudging heavily across the floor to the conference table with his equipment trailing on wheels behind him.

"Good afternoon, my friend. Man, have I got some great clips for you to hear." Rob's excited tone wasn't enough to shake Axel from his funk.

Axel stood and dragged himself to the table. Whipping out a chair, he fell into the seat and leaned back. "Okay, let's go."

Rob cocked his eyebrow. "You're usually talking my ears off and giving me orders before I can sit down." He frowned. "I've never seen you so, so, down. What the hell is wrong with you?"

Axel glanced coolly at his friend, narrowing his eyes and then looked away. "Hmm. Guess I'm out of sorts these days."

Squinting at Axel, "Ah, I know what's going on here," Rob said. "This mood of yours has to be about a woman. Let me guess—that hot little account manager you've been obsessed with for months." He leaned down and pulled out his laptop. "Kerrigan, right?"

Axel grimaced, a frown painting his lips. "Yep." He rested his elbows on the table's surface, his head planted in his hands as he stared off, looking at nothing in particular. "I can't get close to her, and I can't get her off my mind. There's something about this woman, and I can't figure this out. This is…"

Rob grinned. "…this is what every man goes through when he falls."

Like a blow to his gut, Axel's stomach clenched. "Falls?" His eyes were stretched wide. "Oh, no. No. No! If I could get close to her, I'd get her out of my system."

Rob shook his head, gliding his mouse across the slick smooth table. "Man, you've been chasing after the same woman for a year. You haven't been interested in anyone else and you stopped dating."

The truth in Rob's words snapped Axel's head up.

"The fall is scarier than the landing. Believe me." Rob smiled. "Happens to us all. Even you."

Axel pursed his lips. "Man, I'm in trouble. I really do like her. She's amazing." He halted his glare on Rob. "Shit!"

The fall.

***

He stood at her door, hand overhead leaning against the doorframe.

"You ready?" Axel's voice boomed.

Kerrigan jumped in her seat. "Ah! I, I didn't know you were standing there. Yes, I'm ready. I just sent off an email."

"I seem to have a certain startling effect on you. Let's get out of here." Then Axel grinned broadly.

She logged out of her computer, grabbed a stack of folders on the desk, and then claimed her handbag and jacket. She stood up and turned to meet his gaze. One sweeping look at her and he knew he was in trouble. He had deliberately kept his distance from her all day. Seeing her would have heightened his anxiety.

She wore a fitted black knee length dress that hugged the delicate curves of her body accentuating her shapely figure. She had removed her jacket to reveal thin spaghetti straps that clung to her shoulders, and the neckline plunged low enough to reveal a hint of cleavage. Her hair flowed down her back in gracious waves and her caramel skin shimmered flawlessly. His heart melted, and he wouldn't be able to restrain himself much longer.

She looked down quickly, breaking eye contact with him, and shuffled to the door to make her exit. Fixed in the doorway, he turned slightly to let her pass. Attempting to squeeze pass him, her hip lightly grazed his groin, awakening the sleeping giant in his slacks. Molten lava ran through his veins. He didn't attempt to move or apologize.

"Ah." A breathy gasp escaped her lips.

He tensed. "Uh, um." The throaty sound made her jump.

The moment she touched him in the doorway confirmed his plans. Forget professionalism, forget that he was her boss, and forget she'd erected a barrier between them. Tonight, all bets were off. His pride had been wounded when she so coolly rejected him at his admission of feelings for her, but he would proceed with his plan to bring her to her breaking point.

She walked briskly ahead of him after the doorway incident. He didn't mind one bit. He enjoyed the view of her swaying hips and shapely legs. His pulse quickened, and his palms dampened. He chuckled inwardly knowing that she fought to keep her distance from him, and she had been unnerved by what transpired between them. She would receive the surprise of her life for what he had planned. Tonight would be fun.

After exiting the building, she paused. "Aren't you going to lock up the building?" she asked.

"Brenda is here and so are the security officers. Maybe Kevin can lock up."

She frowned, her forehead crinkling in the cute way hers always did. "I forgot to ask where I should meet you."

Looking at her for a moment, and then feeling a twinge of guilt for not being completely forthcoming, he pursed his lips. "You're my date tonight and I'm driving."

"Oh … Okay." The apprehension on her flustered face gave him a rush of excitement. She had no escape.

He opened the passenger door of his black Range Rover and offered his hand to help her climb inside the vehicle. When their hands met, her eyes stretched wide, and a jittery hand fluttered to her throat, but she didn't speak. He strolled around, got inside and started the engine. The melodic sound of a male voice bellowed loudly through the speakers. The next tune that played was the more upbeat and soulful Settle Down track. He hoped she liked his taste in music.

"I wouldn't have pegged you as an Ed Sheeran or Kimbra fan," she said.

"You like them?" Their banter was casual, but at least he was getting to know a little more about her and easing the tension at the same time.

"Yes, I have both of their albums in iTunes," she said.

The corners of his lips curled upward into a grin. "One more thing we have in common."

She turned her head away, staring out of the passenger window as the city life whizzed by. "I guess so," she replied, under her breath with clipped words.

"What?"

"I said, I guess so." She punctuated her words sharply.

He touched her arm. "Sharing things in common isn't so bad."

Conversation between them died down as he merged onto the interstate. She looked to be deep in thought as she fidgeted with her hands. Now that his plan was underway, his nerves heightened.

Finally, breaking the awkward silence, he reached for the volume control on his steering wheel and turned the music down to speak. "Curious about where I'm taking you tonight?"

"Well, I can't say I've given it much thought," she said. He didn't believe her. She must have been racking her brain all day because she had even tried to pry the information from Brenda, who had asked Axel how to respond, when she called requesting information about the evening.

"Really? You haven't wondered at all what I might have up my sleeve. I'm glad you trust me that much." He glanced at her for a moment. "I thought you would want to know what I have planned for us this evening."

He continued his delicious torture, enjoying that she was probably beyond nervous by now, although she would never let on. "Okay, then I'll just surprise you."

"Mr. Christensen, I don't know what you have planned or what kind of meeting you think this is, but I only have intentions to work on a game plan for how we can work together on the McBride account." Her words were stern, and her hands trembled slightly.

He jerked his head toward her, his nostrils flared, heat radiating from his pores as his fiery temper reared. "Now you're back to calling me Mr. Christensen again? Come on, Kerrigan. Don't be childish. You and I are going to spend lots of time together. In the interest of our work, I want you to be comfortable around me."

He took a deep breath and cooled his tone. "Tonight, I have different intentions for you and me that have nothing to do with McBride. I thought we should spend time together. Before the misunderstanding about Misty, you said we needed to talk. I agree. We do need to talk." His eyes never left the road.

"Despite what you wrote in your last email, you and I both know there is something happening between us. I feel it, and I know you do too. You have no reason to be afraid of this or me," he said, waving his hands between them. "I want you to trust me. I don't want to hurt you."

She glanced up at him briefly, and then looked away, staring into the early evening sky. "You don't *want* to hurt me, but if I don't give you an opportunity to, then I'll be sure you won't. Now please just take me back to work. There's no point to this evening."

"I'm sorry, Kerrigan, but that's not going to happen. Tonight is about us, and you're coming with me. Remember that elephant you insist on ignoring? Well, our feelings are feeding him and he's grown too large to ignore. Time to face the elephant."

She swallowed hard, averted his gaze, but didn't say another word.

Fifteen minutes later, he pulled up to an estate home with a gated entrance. The gates glided across the metal tracks and opened, and the SUV continued down a long driveway, which led to beautiful gardens graced by the presence of a magnificent house. One of the bays of the three-car garage opened and he pulled inside. She looked over at him and her mouth dropped open, her face painted with panic.

CHAPTER ELEVEN

Oh my god! I'm at Axel Christensen's house. Kerrigan's chest tightened, and she couldn't breathe. The tension between them had been mounting, and she managed to push him away, but she never expected him to resort to an act of desperation this bold and daring.

The large heavy garage door screeched closed, and pitch-blackness surrounded them. Kerrigan couldn't see anything, her eyes wide and searching. Her heart pounded so hard, she knew he could hear the hard thud against her chest. Cold air blew from the vent, sending a shiver up her spine and the goose bumps that had risen on her arms multiplied. Wrapping her arms around herself, she shielded herself from the arctic blast and him. "I assume this is where you live. Why are we at your house? Did you forget something here?" she asked hastily, the nervous tension clinging to the end of her words sounded louder in the dark.

He opened the driver's side door, cut off the engine and faced her. The overhead light cast an eerie glow. "I need to be alone with you. I thought we could enjoy dinner. My housekeeper Emma rivals some of the best gourmet chefs in town." He covered her folded hands resting in her lap and gently caressed her fingers. The sensation of his touch made her tingle from her fingertips, flowed through her core and down to her feet. She stopped breathing. She wished he didn't affect her that way.

"And, I thought you could use a little fun. You work much too hard. You're always the first one in and the last one to leave."

She frowned at him, her forehead furrowed—a question held in her eyes. "Axel, I…"

He continued, halting her words. "I pay attention to everything you do. You told me that you moved here for a change. I won't let you slip back into bad habits."

His concern penetrated her heart. "I appreciate your looking out for me."

The tone of his voice softened, and his eyes burrowed into her flesh. "I also hoped we could spend some time together getting to know each other a little more, talking—just talking."

Despite his protective nature, the danger warning in her mind rang out like a storm siren signaling impending disaster. "I thought we were already getting to know each other. I don't understand why you're doing this."

"I want us do something together that isn't work-related. We had fun hanging out at the baseball game. This is for us both." Although he spoke with confidence, his words came out winded, his knee bounced restlessly, and his eyes darkened with an intensity she hadn't seen before. Unmasked, his anxiety took the form of perspiration lightly glistening across his forehead. He shifted in his seat. "And, because I don't want you on the roads so late at night, I've arranged the guest suite for you to sleep here overnight. I'll take you back to the office tomorrow for your car."

She swallowed hard. "Axel, I don't know what to say. Do I have any choice?" *Okay Kerrigan, Axel wants you. Breathe. Don't panic.*

He lifted her hand and brought it to his lips, dusting it tenderly with a kiss. "Kerrigan, you always have a choice. I just want you to give me a chance. Dinner is ready. Let's go eat. I know you're uncomfortable. If you're still feeling unsure after dinner, I'll drive you home tonight and send for your car tomorrow."

"Just one question, is this how you treat all the special ladies in your life?" she asked.

His blue eyes sparkled magnificently drawing her in. "You're the only lady in my life. I want you, Kerrigan, no one else." Axel spoke so definitively and sincerely that his words jolted her. He offered no further explanation or apology, simply stated his feelings as fact.

The driver's door flung open wider, and then slammed shut. He bolted to her side and offered his hand to help her out. She couldn't believe he had gone through such great lengths, to spend time alone with her, but if he thought he was getting lucky tonight, he would be sorely mistaken—blue balls and all.

Still stunned, she followed him down the hall. A heavenly aroma greeted them on the way to the kitchen. As they made their entrance, she glanced around noticing the expensive solid oak cabinetry stained in deep chocolate contrasted by nickel hardware. The glass tile backsplash added character, and a pop of color with its vibrant teal, green and blue toned hues.

An older woman who grabbed Kerrigan in a tight embrace before she could object greeted them.

"Welcome, Kerrigan!" The woman spoke her name without introduction.

The warmth of the woman's hug, although unexpected, eased some of her tension away, the familiar feeling like the safety of a mother's embrace. She stiffened realizing that becoming too comfortable could be hazardous.

Releasing her, the woman placed her hands on Kerrigan's arms, eased back and studied her face. "Oh! Axel, she's as lovely as you said. It's so good to meet you. I'm Emma. Axel says the nicest things about you all the time."

Axel closed his eyes tightly and winced. It had never occurred to her that this strong, confident and domineering man could embarrass, but there it was riddled across his face. She didn't know what to make of this interaction, this night of strange surprises. Slowly, he opened one eye at a time and rejoined them.

"It's nice to meet you too, Emma," she said, with a question in her voice. "He says nice things about me?" She glanced at Axel again and smiled. She enjoyed seeing this side of him.

Axel's face turned to stone. "Yes, I make it a point to talk about all my employees and what's happening at work."

"He truly does dear. But you, you hold a special place in his heart." Emma gave Kerrigan a wink.

He grabbed her forearm and tugged her toward another doorway, yelling over his shoulder to Emma as they left. "Okay! We're heading to the dining room now. Kerrigan has had a long day, so let's get her fed," Axel said, his tone gruff.

Axel made it clear that he wanted to spend time alone with her and break down the barriers between them. Now, trapped in his house, forced to spend an entire evening with the man, she would have no refuge from her emotions or from him.

She was perplexed and had more questions than answers. What was it about him that drove her to the brink of insanity? Why couldn't she have been attracted to a reasonable man who was safe? Was she a glutton for punishment? Sure they shared more things in common than they had differences, he made her laugh, he was kind and gentle yet firm and commanding when he felt the need to take charge, and he was hot as hell. Why did she have to be attracted to the only man who was certain to break her heart? He was everything she wanted, but not anything she needed.

Dazzled, she shuffled from one foot to the other. "May I wash up first?" she asked.

He gently placed his hand on the small of her back and led her down a hallway. "Yes, of course. The restroom is the first door on the left." A slow crooked smile crept onto his lips while his eyes skimmed her over. "I'll be in the dining room."

As soon as she closed the door, she covered her face with her hands. *Oh my god! Damn Ashley for being right about everything! What should I do?* He was after her. With that knowledge, her stomach twisted, legs went weak, and heart beat wildly inside her chest. Under normal circumstances, she would have taken the time to note the charming character of the restroom, but this situation was anything but normal.

She did the only thing that made sense to her at the time, and she had to act quickly. An escape through the window wasn't an option. Her hands glided over the curve of her hips. The women on her mother's side of the family always prattled about being stacked with hips that could catch a man and birth his babies. The joke didn't seem so funny now. Anchored against a wall, she pulled out her cell phone from her handbag and dialed Ashley.

Ashley answered on the second ring. "Hey, Kerri."

Kerrigan whispered into the phone's speaker. "Ash, please just listen. No jokes right now okay? I'm in a predicament, and I need your advice," she pleaded.

"Aren't you out with Axel right now? What? Let me guess. You're in his bed trying to decide which position he should have you in first," her tone indicating her amusement at Kerrigan's heightened state of mania.

She couldn't find the right words, and she didn't know exactly how to explain her situation. "Close enough. Didn't I tell you that he wanted to discuss our work relationship?"

"Yeah, so?"

"Well, he lied." Speaking in rapid clipped sentences, she whispered as much of the evening's events in incoherent fashion, starting with what happened in the office. "I think he wanted me to know he was aroused. He didn't apologize, and he didn't even seem embarrassed." Ashley cackled so loudly that Kerrigan had to mute the phone until she was done. "Kerri, what did you expect the man to say, 'sorry, you gave me a hard on'?" Ashley laughed again.

Kerrigan rolled her eyes. "It wasn't professional behavior."

"Uh, I don't think Axel is very interested in behaving professionally with you. I think he's interested in X-rated behavior with you."

Sinking to the floor in a squat, she let her frustration bleed through the phone. "Ash, I'm at his house right now, and I'm freaking out. What should I do?"

"So, you really *do* want to know which position he should have you in first," Ashley said and then snorted.

"No! Cut it out, Ash! He kidnapped me. I have to get out of here. I can't fit through this damn window. The hallway opens into the foyer across from the dining room, where he's waiting for me. Even if I managed to sneak pass, an alarm might sound when I open the door. Plus, I don't think I could propel the metal security gate. Do you think he has watch dogs?" Her voice trembled, on the verge of tears.

"Okay. Okay. Okay. Kerri, you need to calm down. The man likes you. His attraction to you isn't that terrible. Is it? Actually, I think it's romantic. Just go with it. You're freaking out because you like him too. I don't think Axel is the type to force you to do anything you don't want to do."

Getting up from her squat, she stood, and paced the bathroom floor. "I just don't know what to do or say. I can barely speak around him. I'm a bumbling idiot. Oh, why is this happening?" She pressed her right hand against her forehead.

"First of all, I hate you and so does every single woman who has ever laid their eyes on Axel Christensen. Secondly, stop thinking. Go with your heart. I'd tell you to go with another part of your anatomy, but I have a feeling that will happen soon enough."

"This isn't funny. I'm terrified."

"Kerri, relax. He's just a man who likes you. Granted he's fine-as-hell, smart and super rich, but underneath it all, he's a vulnerable man like all the rest. Be yourself and stop calling me."

She closed her eyes, took a deep breath, and then exhaled slowly. "Okay. Thanks, Ash. If you don't hear from me again, just remember where I told I'd been taken."

"Kerri, you're crazy. Now go get some of Axel's rod! Goodbye." Ashley laughed again as she hung up.

She appreciated her friend, but sometimes Ashley was simply too much. Kerrigan stared at her reflection in the mirror. What did he see in her? She washed her hands and fixed her hair. Taking another deep breath, she opened the bathroom door and walked out, heading toward the dining room.

***

Axel was seated when Kerrigan approached. He stood as soon as she made her entrance. He appreciated seeing her walk into the room in all her flustered glory. Pulling out the tufted parsons chair next to his, he held out his hand to help her into the seat. She tried to withdraw her small trembling hand from his immediately. He wrapped his fingers tightly around hers; firmly clutching her delicate hand so that she couldn't escape, and then he looked into her eyes. Those hazel eyes—he could get lost in them. The moment was surreal, one that he had fantasized about so many times in the past year that he wondered if she were actually there. When she blinked, it jolted him back to reality. A rush of excitement and jittery nerves coursed through his gut, as though someone had just knocked the wind out of him. The feeling passed in an instant, and he regained control of his emotions.

His gaze ran the length of her slender, shapely form, and then met her eyes again. "You look absolutely stunning." He caressed her fingers. "Kerrigan, I'm sorry. I know this isn't the evening you had in mind, but you don't have to be afraid of me."

"No, this isn't the evening I had in mind at all, and my better judgment tells me fear is good." The cold tone and pitch of her voice made his heart sink.

He brought her hand to his heart. "I promise not to do anything you don't want me to do. May I be completely honest with you?"

"Please, because I don't think I can take any more surprises." She yanked her hand away from him, and he allowed her this, realizing her discomfort.

"You know I'd be lying if I said I wasn't extremely attracted to you, Kerrigan. We've worked together for a year now. In the past few months, I've gotten to know you enough to know that I really like you. You're very special to me, and I want to get to know you even better. I couldn't think of what else to do."

She needed to know how he felt. Perhaps his vulnerability would penetrate her walls. "I thought I was finally breaking through to you, but after my email when I revealed my feelings for you, you went as cold as ice. I couldn't wait until Saturday. I came home early to see you." He lifted his eyes in surrender to her. "I can't explain what I'm feeling, but I also don't want to fight this anymore and I won't let you fight this either—there's strong chemistry between us, not like anything I've ever felt. I want us to explore our feelings. Will you give us a chance to find out if there's more?" With a simple yes or no, he gave her power to ignite or crush him.

"I don't understand. I'm not your type." He hadn't expected her to say that.

He frowned. "What do you mean?" Leaning in closer, he watched as the room's light flickered, shimmering against her caramel skin that appeared brushed with diamond dust. Her breasts rose and fell as her chest heaved.

"I've seen some of the beautiful models you've traipsed in and out of the office. I'm not interested in being your flavor of the month or another notch on your bedpost." Her words were like a mirror, reflecting his whorish behavior and he didn't like the image he cast.

"Fair. I've dated many women, but that's all. You can't believe every rumor you hear about me. Most of those dates were one-time events. I usually never even see those women after the first date."

She toyed with the white cloth napkin in her lap. Fiery eyes seared Axel's smoldering gaze. "Wow! Is that supposed to convince me? One-night stands and then you're done—every girl's dream."

He shook his head. "That's not what I meant. I just date. I don't do one-night stands, Kerrigan. Most of those women threw themselves at me, which was quite a turn-off and I rejected their advances. I won't lie to you. I did sleep with a few of them."

"It's never wise to mix business with pleasure. Axel, what happens when you tire of me?" She spewed in rapid-fire secession.

"What makes you think I would tire of you? That wouldn't happen. I haven't dated a single woman in nearly a year because of you." His stomach churned. She should have been in his arms by now, with his lips pressed to her plump ones.

"Mr. Christensen, that's noble, but don't cease your extracurricular activities on account of me." Her words cut into him. Like a man in need of a tourniquet—he had to stop the bleeding.

This wasn't how he wanted the conversation to continue. "Kerrigan, like you, I'm made of flesh and bone, and I'm easily wounded," he said, switching gears. "Can we behave civilly—stop throwing daggers just this once and enjoy an evening together?" he asked, his eyes pleading with her.

Glancing down into her napkin-covered lap, "Axel, I, I'm … okay. I'll try," she stammered.

"Thank you. I only want to get to know you better." He paused, his lips curling upward. "So tell me, when was your last relationship, Miss Mulls?" he asked.

"It's been a while."

He frowned in puzzlement. "That's surprising. You're beautiful, accomplished, intelligent and independent. Surely someone has tried to snatch you up by now."

"The same could be said about you, Mr. Christensen. Except, while I'm accomplished, you're super successful. Why are you single?"

"Miss Mull, you think I'm beautiful?" he asked, deliberately flashing his most dangerous smile eclipsed by a serious stone-like expression. "I guess I'm still single because I hadn't met the right woman, until now."

A crimson glow touched her caramel-toned cheeks. "What makes you think I'm the right woman?"

He stared into her. "I like that you speak your mind, and you challenge me. You're beautiful inside and out. You have a kind heart and gentle spirit. We like the same music and movies, work in the same industry, share a love of the outdoors, find the same things funny, and I can't get you off my mind. I love the way you smell, and I love it when we touch. No other woman has ever made me feel the way you do." His palms dampened, and his throat closed up.

She blushed again but had no response.

***

Their conversation died down as dinner was presented—roast duck, grilled asparagus, and baked herb potato wedges served with Pinot Noir. Kerrigan lightly picked over the meal set in front of her. She looked forward to dinner, but the situation she found herself in made her forget her hunger.

Taken aback by the events of the evening and Axel's confession, she needed a distraction from her feelings and inner musings. Her eyes danced around, admiring the dining room's grandness and blend of styles. The upper half of the walls wore a bold graphic print. The background of the wallpaper was a soft neutral color covered by a swirly pattern of deep gray dotted lines accented by organic shapes in tones of turquoise and gold flecks interspersed throughout.

"What do you think of the room?" he asked as if he wanted her approval, which was odd. Axel didn't seem to care what anyone thought of his decisions.

Her eyes darted around the room again. "The décor is contemporary and elegant, and at the same time, very eclectic. I like it."

A faint smile crossed his lips, but his express was one she couldn't place.

She shifted in her seat and then tilted her head back. A chandelier hung above them from the ten-foot-high coffered ceiling, the accessory unlike any other she had seen. Blown translucent crystal had been designed into a quagmire of organic shapes that complemented the pattern of the exquisite wallpaper.

"I love how the chandelier seems to float in mid-air. The light bounces off the gold flecks in the wallpaper." She hadn't expected any room in his home to be so warm and romantic, not that she had ever given much thought to the interior of his home.

His smile was soft. Almost timid, that was a first. "Inspired by Chihuly. Do you know his work?"

Her heart pounded, and mouth became dry. "Yes, he's one of my favorite artists." She reached for her glass and took a long sip.

Mimicking, he raised his glass, swirled the wine around and sipped, his eyes never leaving hers. "Hmm. Something else we…"

"…share in common," she said, finishing his statement. Turning away from his stare, heat rushed to her cheeks.

A crooked smirk perched his lips, then spread to a full grin. "I'd love to show you the rest of the house tomorrow."

"Sure, I'd like to see it."

His eyes followed her gaze. "You've barely touched your food. Don't you like it?" he asked and cocked his head to the side.

"The food is excellent. I'm not hungry … just can't eat much right now." Attempting to appease her host, she took a bite of potatoes and continued scanning the room.

The hardwood floors were stained in deep chocolate, a nice contrast to the stark whiteness of the wainscot paneling that ran around the lower half of the walls. A large buffet stood against one wall while the opposite wall was a set of French doors flanked by golden silk drapes that pooled to the floor.

"Those doors lead to a terrace overlooking the grounds that you saw on the drive up to the house." He sipped his wine again.

The room was masculine and vibrant but full of passion and warmth, like the man who sat there with his perfectly sculpted features in his white dress shirt, muscles bulging, threatening her sanity. She liked the room, and she liked him.

"You have phenomenal design sensibility. This room is definitely a one-of-a-kind masterpiece," she complimented.

"Thank you. My taste in women is equally exquisite. I covet one-of-a-kind treasures."

Although his words touched her heart, she didn't know if they held any permanence. Were his feelings being driven by his desire to bed her? The thought infuriated her.

"You're a collector?" she asked, an icy twinge beneath her words.

"Of sorts."

"Well, I'm not an acquisition."

His shoulders stiffened. Slowly, the line stretched across his face relaxed, his lips curled upward. "I'm a collector of fine art, not women." His smug grin irritated her. "Put up all the defenses and excuses you want, but that won't change how I feel."

Nervous waves rolled in her stomach. "This is dangerous."

"What's dangerous? The fact that I want you or that you want me too, or what can happen when you put two people who are wildly attracted to each other in a romantic room alone?"

Placing her hand against the table's edge, she attempted to push away. He grabbed her wrist and held her tight. "We can't happen," she protested.

His grip tightened. "We will happen."

Lowering her head, she turned away. A single tear leaked from the corner of her eye. She dabbed the moisture dry before he noticed.

"Axel, I can't let this happen." Her small voice fraught, tears pooled in her eyes threatened to spills.

He released her wrist. "Kerrigan, some things are beyond your control."

She was completely attracted to the man in a way she had never experienced before. With Axel sitting next to her, she wasn't sure of herself. *Stop thinking. Go with your heart.* Ashley's words came crashing into her consciousness. She had promised to open herself to new experiences. Could she, should she let go for once and give in to temptation?

***

Axel saw a tear slide down her cheek. The pit of his gut dropped. He placed his folk down on the plate with a clink and turned to face her. "Kerrigan, let's just take things slowly. I realize you're hesitant. I know you're scared. I want to earn your trust. Just try to relax. As I've already told you, I'm willing to be patient, especially because you're worth the wait."

She adjusted the napkin on her lap, avoiding his eyes. "Please understand that this is overwhelming to me, the very last thing I ever expected."

Softening his tone, he hoped to soothe her anxiety. "I understand, but I know I'm right, you know I'm right. I know you feel the connection too. I can't stop thinking about you. I just want to be near you."

"Is this your idea of taking things slowly? Axel, just a few weeks ago I thought of you as my boss and I never imagined anything more. I had no other intentions or thoughts about you otherwise. Now you're telling me that we should explore the chemistry that you think exists between us and …"

Before she could finish her lecture, he stood, grabbed her by the hand and pulled her up from the table.

"Axel, what are you doing?"

He didn't say a word, only looked at her intensely, and then led her out onto the terrace. She was stunned into silence. When they reached the wrought iron railing, he released her. They faced each other in stillness, their eyes locked. With the sudden urge to consume her, his burly hands spanned her tiny waist and drew her closer, bringing her into full contact with his body.

"Axel, what, what are you doing?" she asked again, and again, he stared at her in silence.

He liked the way she quivered under his touch. He wouldn't let her break his grip, even if she protested. He knew she didn't want him to let her go. His left hand caressed her cheek as he stared deeply into her hazel eyes—beautiful eyes that stared up at him blinking rapidly and fighting tears.

Towering above her, he leaned down slowly, relishing her smell and feel of her pressed against him, and whispered in her ear. "Baby, this ends now. I won't let you fight this anymore." He crushed his lips against hers with such fierce passion that a whimper escaped her soul, and she collapsed into him.

His tongue invaded her mouth, taking and giving pleasure. A raspy growl escaped his lips as he devoured her voraciously. He had dreamed of this moment for so long and now here she was in his arms. She tasted like sweet honey, better than he had ever imaged. He pulled her closer, wrapping her in his warm embrace, their bodies taut and flush. He stole her breath making it hard for her to remain coherent. His tongue danced inside her mouth tangoing with hers. He was hungry for her, licking and sucking her lips so passionately that she released a soft moan. She trembled at his touch, but he steadied her in his arms.

The heat between them rose, as did his masculine desire. His erection pressed hard against her stomach begging entrance into her womanhood. The palms of her hands planted squarely against his chiseled chest. He savored her fingertips as they glided over every ridge and valley of his strength. She clung to him as if he were required for her own fortitude, kissing him fervently.

The ferociousness of his kiss tamed after several minutes, becoming more sensual and less hedonistic. He took his time admiring her, how she felt beneath his touch, how she responded to his stroke. He had yearned to touch every part of her for so long that he couldn't control his greedy hands. They were like an octopus. One hand cupped her round behind while the other hand caressed her cheek tenderly. Then Axel's hand crept slowly up her arm, eager fingers dancing across her shoulders while the other hand slid across her breast. With both hands, he adjusted the tilt of her head to deepen his kiss, running his fingers through her long hair.

He felt the rapid rise and fall of her chest against his. A delicate hand gripped his shirt, gathering folds of white fabric between trembling fingers, the other lifted to his face caressed him tenderly. She breathed heavily and unsteadily. The way her body responded to his, he was certain that in that moment if he wanted to, he could make love to her beneath the naked starry night sky. He wanted her, but not like this. He respected and cared for her too much to cheapen their first time together. She deserved to be cherished slowly and sensually. He wanted to take his time and worship every part of her, and he did.

Ten minutes had passed before he pried his lips from hers. With his eyes still closed, and his breathing ragged, he placed his head down into the crook of her neck, breathing her in. She threw her head back and released a tiny sigh. The world spun around them, and her knees buckled as the haze of sexual frenzy slowly wafted away. He caught her in his arms and pulled her closer to keep her balanced on her feet. She still trembled in his clutch.

"You all right, baby?"

She kept her head down, her eyes avoiding his. He knew she was embarrassed. Barely audible, she managed one word. "Yes."

"Look at me, Kerrigan." He demanded. When she didn't comply, he lifted her chin and looked deeply into her eyes. "Can you deny it now? I felt your passion, and I know you felt mine."

Her large and round eyes were captured by his gaze like a doe trapped by its hunter. “No.” Her response was timid.

He searched her eyes as a single tear escaped and trickled down her cheek. Taking the pad of his thumb, he wiped the tear away. “Baby, you’re okay. You’re safe with me. I would never hurt you. You drive me mad, unlike any other woman ever has. I want you, no one else—just you, Kerrigan.”

Her small shivering hand in his, he led her inside the house and up the stairs. No other words were spoken between them, and he guided her down the hall toward the bedroom like a lamb eager and willing to be slaughtered, and served up as the main course.

CHAPTER TWELVE

Axel wanted her badly. Tonight proved Kerrigan wanted him with equal hunger. She had been an indulgent fantasy for so long and now here she was in his home, in his arms and at his mercy. He knew that doubts and fear filled her. He had to do it now.

He stopped outside of the bedroom door and released her hand.

"This is the guest suite. If you need anything tonight, Emma's number is on the nightstand and my bedroom is the last one down the hall."

"Oh. I thought you wanted to…"

"Believe me—I want to so badly that I'm in pain. I'm tempted to walk pass this door and take you to my bedroom. My feelings for you are serious, Kerrigan, and I want to take things slowly for both our sakes. I respect you too much. You okay with that?"

She beamed and exhaled the breath she had been holding. "More than okay. Thank you." This was the first time she seemed to relax that evening.

Stepping forward, he backed her against the door and placed his hands on either side of her head, and then leaned in.

"Don't get the wrong idea, Kerrigan. I want you in my bed, and I will have you, but not like this and not tonight. I won't make any apologies for wanting you or for what I plan to do to you."

Kerrigan's shoulders slumped, and her body sank into the molded panel door. Her timid gaze and those large round eyes made his blood heat. Damn, he wanted her. She whispered a soft, "Oh."

His arms dropped to his side, and then he backed away. His eyes traced her curvy frame, slow and sensual, and her face turned crimson. He hadn't meant to intimidate her, but he liked that he could turn up the heat within her. The kiss was a major victory, but he knew other battles lie ahead.

"We have a full day tomorrow. You better rest up baby. There are new clothes in the wardrobe that should fit you. I hope you like them."

Her forehead wrinkled. "I thought you were taking me back to the office tomorrow."

"I'll take you back tomorrow evening. I want you all to myself for most of the day. Besides, I still owe you a tour. Do you have better plans or a hot date?"

"I do have chores and errands to run on Saturday, and no, I don't have a hot date, not that my plans are any of your business."

"Sorry, sweetheart. You belong to me tomorrow." *And forever.* "Unless your errands are a matter of life or death, they will have to wait. Take Monday, Tuesday and Wednesday off, if you need to, but tomorrow you're with me. For the record, you are my business. No more dates for you, unless you're going out with me."

He smiled, caressed her cheek with the back of his hand, and then pecked her tenderly on the lips. "I can't sleep now. I'm going to burn off some energy. Goodnight, Kerrigan." He turned to walk away.

"Goodnight," she said sheepishly. "Thank you for the clothes." Her reply, a subtle whisper.

Glancing back at her one last time, Axel could see his future with the woman in the doorway.

***

Kerrigan walked into the room, and then closed the door behind her. Instinctively, she twisted the little button on the knob, locking the door. Without looking around at her surroundings, she made her way to the bed and tossed herself onto the crisp white linens, rolling and giddy like a sixteen-year-old girl after her first kiss. Her legs still felt like soft spaghetti and her head spun. She lay daydreaming, eyes fixed to the ceiling as she mulled over the kiss she had just shared with Axel. She floated high in a state of bliss and then came back down to earth, sitting up, she glanced around and observed the magnificent room, chic with clean lines and minimalistic furnishings in mahogany toned woods.

There were many thoughts racing through Kerrigan's mind. She had been kissed before, but never like that, never to the point that her legs were limp, her mind blank and her desire built so strong that she couldn't breathe and was ready to surrender. The question that haunted her, that tormented her to no end was what would happen if she gave in to Axel.

Deciding on a shower, she looked through the grand wardrobe for a change of clothes. She found that all the clothing was indeed her size just as he had said they would be. She also noted that there were enough clothes for more than one night's stay. How long did he plan to keep her there? She took a fresh set of undergarments, a seductive nightgown and robe, and made her way to the bathroom.

Like everything else in Axel's home, the bathroom was unbelievable, like a room come to life from the pages of an upscale interior design magazine. The room's spa-like qualities included expensive stone flooring and a soft pale green color palette, making the setting serene and comforting.

She turned on the shower. Steam quickly filled the room, easing her tension and muddled thoughts. The warm water cascaded down her body as she reminisced about Axel's lips on hers only moments earlier. His strong commanding hands roaming her body had been the fulfillment of her fantasies. The memories conjured the same sensation and warmth between Kerrigan's thighs.

She ran her hands down her stomach and to her hot, throbbing sex. Rubbing vigorously at her clitoris, she imagined he was touching her. The pressure was mounted on top of remnants of the evening's earlier events. She climaxed almost as soon as she touched herself. It was quick, but she needed to release the sexual tension that had been building all night—heck, all year. She wasn't into masturbation, but he had done something to stir the hunger inside her. It wasn't an earth-shattering orgasm, but she felt better afterwards.

She slipped on the sexy nightgown, combed her hair and headed for the balcony through French doors dressed with light, ivory curtains. The breeze was invigorating in the darkness that loomed around her. The only light illuminating the night was the cerulean glow of the pool below. She barely could see anything on the large balcony, but she managed to find a lounge chair and sank into the seat. She would use this time to organize her sparse thoughts.

If anyone had told her that she would be at her boss' house making out with him on Friday evening and spending the night, she would have burst into a fit of laughter. This was certainly one hell of a start to opening herself to new adventures and experiences. Intellectually, she knew the risks of getting involved with Axel, but she wanted him despite the high stakes.

She was about to head inside when a bright light emanating from a set of glass doors caught her attention. The back of the house was u-shaped, and the glass doors were opposite her room on the lower level of the house. She stilled as she focused, making out a figure of a person, a man—Axel. He came into clearer view. With his back facing the door and the balcony being so dark, he wouldn't see her watching him. He lifted and removed his shirt, exposing all his manly appeal. His body was sculpted to the hilt. He dropped to the ground and began a set of pushups. Even from this view, she could see every muscle in his strong arms and back, flex and strain at his rigorous exertion.

She salivated at the sight of him. She wanted to know what it would feel like to lie underneath him, feeling the sensation of his body thrusting into hers. She shook the thought out of her head as quickly as it had come. He finally stood, stretched his arms outward and then made his way to what looked like a treadmill. Now he was facing in her direction. She jumped up and headed for the opened door to her room, nearly crashing into a table on her way in. She ran inside and closed the door before he could catch her. Her heart pounded heavily against her chest. That was close.

She was restless. Lying in bed, Kerrigan allowed her heart rate and breathing to normalize. Twenty minutes had passed since she had come back inside, and it was almost eleven o'clock. Ashley would still be awake, so she decided to give her a call. She picked up her phone and began looking through her recent calls, to redial the number, when suddenly there was light rapping on her bedroom door. Axel? No, couldn't be. When she peeked through the French doors five minutes ago, he was still working out downstairs. She wrapped the robe around her loosely, walked toward the sound and pulled open the door. Her jaw nearly hit the floor when she saw him standing in front of her shirtless, his body glistening in the low light cast from the room. His right arm extended over his head with his hand resting on the doorframe.

He leaned in with his head cocked to one side. "Enjoy the show?" he asked with a smug grin.

She was busted. A surge of heat radiated across her sun-kissed face, and she knew her caramel pigment wouldn't be enough to hide the redness that colored her cheeks.

He delighted in her torture as he continued, and the intonation of his voice even more seductive now. "I saw you out on the balcony watching me. Did you like what you saw?"

The warm glow of light coming from the room and bending around the peaks and valleys of his cut torso incited her senses and libido. Her heart rate increased, and her eyes widened as she watched a single bead of sweat slink its way from the nape of his neck, across his shoulder and down to his heaving chest. She was barely able to find words. "I, I'm sorry. I needed some air. I didn't mean to." Forming a thought was hard enough, let alone completing an entire sentence with Axel standing in the doorway nearly buff. She hated that this man affected her this way.

He leaned into the room more. "Kerrigan, you still haven't answered my question. Should I come in and get the answer from you?"

"Yes. No! I mean, yes I enjoyed …. I did watch you, but I didn't mean to, and no, you shouldn't come in," she managed to stammer out.

Don't cry. He's only fooling around. Don't cry. She told herself.

He extended his left arm up, placing his other hand onto to the other side of the doorframe. Her breathing quickened. Her gaze traveled his body, insatiable. His gray sweat pants hung low on his waist, exposing the sculpted V-shape of his lower abdomen, and they did nothing to camouflage the massive bulge in his pants.

That damn grin was planted on his face, as though he knew she was feasting on his body. "Miss Mulls, you sure you don't want me to come inside? I'll gladly give you your very own private show," he said even more seductively.

"No, please don't. I'm sorry. It happened so quickly, I really didn't mean to." Her eyes felt heavy as tears filled them.

He studied her for a minute, eyebrows turning downward. As if realizing his offense, he backed off immediately. Lowering his arms, he took a less menacing stance. "Baby, I didn't mean to upset you. I'm cruel. You were on my mind. When I saw you on the balcony, I knew you were still awake. I wanted to see you one more time before going to bed."

She didn't expect what happened next. He grabbed her, pulling her into his warm embrace. She willingly went, and tears trickled slowly down Kerrigan's cheeks. She reacted like an immature baby in his arms. "I'm not a voyeur or some weird peeping tom," she murmured into his slick chest. "I'm sorry I watched you. I do like you Axel, but I need to take things slowly, please. I just get so nervous when you're around that I don't know what to do with myself. You scare me," she sobbed and pleaded. Her head pressed into his naked glistening torso as her tears spilled down the hard ridges of his chest.

"I know baby. I'm a terrible tease. I'm sorry I upset you. This is new territory for me too. You drive me crazy, and then I lose control. Since you came to work for me, I've been watching you every day, and you have no idea how badly I want you. I don't want to frighten you. I want you to trust me. We can take things slowly, but remember, I'm a man who knows what he wants and I go after it. I've wanted you since the day I met you."

She calmed down, her sobs quieting. His words were beautiful and made her heart sing. With his hand gently placed under her chin, he tilted her face up so that their gazes met. Sweeping his thumbs gently underneath her eyes, he wiped away her tears.

"You okay now?" he asked, and then kissed her tenderly on the forehead. His lips lingered there for a few moments, and he stepped back to put distance between them.

"More than okay. Give me some time to get to know you more, to learn to trust you," she said softly.

Her loosely wrapped robe had sprung open, exposing the sexy red nightgown she wore underneath it. Axel stepped back further.

His eyes swept over her body. The ravenous look he gave unnerved her was as if she were the most luscious, temptress on the earth. "I'll take you whenever you're ready to have me. Goodnight, Kerrigan. Lock your door." He took three broad steps backwards to make his retreat.

She quaked inside, the desire blazing in his eyes the inducement. "Goodnight, Axel. I will."

***

Saturday, September 22

After a refreshing shower, Kerrigan tossed herself onto the bed and called Ashley. She confided in her, sharing every detail of the night before. Ashley was supportive and encouraging, not even once making light of her circumstance with one of her typical smart-alecky quips.

"Kerri, you really like him, don't you?"

"Yes." Kerrigan paused and inhaled a deep breath. "But, I'm afraid of what it means and of what he wants."

"What do you mean? Are you afraid of getting hurt?"

"Yes, of course. The man can have any woman he wants. I wonder if his fascination with me is driven by something else, sexualizing me because I'm a black woman. I wonder if I'm an experiment."

"Kerri, that's something you two need to discuss. Just because he's attracted to you, doesn't make him the bad guy. He's a man and you're a woman, and when there's chemistry like you two seem to have, that naturally leads to … well, you know what that leads to."

"Thank you, Ash. I'm just so inexperienced at this relationship stuff. You know I have a horrible track record with men. What happens if he breaks my heart?"

"What happens if he doesn't? I know I talk a lot of crap about Axel, but don't doom yourself to be hurt before you give yourself a chance to be loved."

Her toes dug into the soft pile, feet planted firmly on the carpet, and she stood. "I hope it's not too late. Thanks again, Ash. I'll call you later." Her cell phone went down on the wooden nightstand with a light thump.

One hand twisted the doorknob. Kerrigan's throat suddenly dry, shaky legs carried her on impulse into the hallway and downstairs, moist palms sliding across the banister.

***

Axel sat behind his desk, his attention captured by his computer screen. The door opened, and a light tapping sound pulled his attention away from his monitor. He swiveled his chair around, looked up, and drank her in with his eyes. *God, she's beautiful.* He loved the way the spaghetti strap of her yellow dress hung slightly off her left shoulder with tendrils of her hair flowing over its naked skin. He motioned her to come inside the room. She made her way toward him. Without saying a word, he stood, walked to the other side of the large oak desk and stopped in front of her.

Her lips parted as though she was about to speak. He didn't want to talk. Stepping closer to her, their bodies were nearly touching. Her words halted, she stood in silence looking up at him, and then lowered her head. Anxiety hid behind those beautiful eyes, and he imagined she needed to escape his heated gaze.

Since their sensual kiss on the balcony, he hadn't been able to think of much else. It would take another bold act on his part to reignite that flame, and he wasn't at a loss for what to do next. He wrapped his fingers around her left wrist and moved her hand behind her back, pinning it against the small of her waist. Her head lifted, and her eyes found his, widening as a subtle gasp escaped her lips. He grabbed her other wrist and pinned it behind her, and then pulled her into him. With his arms swaddling her and their bodies pressed together, he could feel her heart beat wildly.

She didn't put up a fight, or protest—only searched his eyes with her soft round ones, timid and willing to surrender herself to him completely. He tilted his head down and covered her lips with his. The second he tasted her supple lips, every inch of him warmed and his stomach tightened. Fueled by raw masculine desire and a rush of testosterone, he devoured her sweet, tender kiss with the savagery of his rough, invading tongue, dipping in and out of her mouth, his lips sucking hers voraciously.

He released her wrists and pulled her closer, allowing him to deepen their kiss. His hands slid from her waist, then to her behind cupping and kneading her firm roundness. He tightened his embrace and felt her small trembling hands against his chest. Knowing that he affected her in his way excited him to the brink of no return. Their bodies collided in a fit of passionate rage. He backed her into the desk so forcefully that she stumbled onto it, planting her into a seated position on its edge. Her hands gripped his biceps, steadying her quivering body. Their lips remained locked, each one breathless and aching with want for the other. He wedged himself between her legs, opening her wide to receive this girth.

"Axel, I … I…" She whispered sweetly, managing to break the possessive hold he had over her mouth. "Axel?" She moaned softly.

His name coming from her lips rang like music to his ears. "Hmm." The guttural groan escaped his lips.

Pressed hard against his sweat pants, his erection threatened to pierce through and thrust into her moisture. He shifted his position to make use of his eager fingers. His hand slowly massaged her knee and made its way to her inner thigh—his fingers eager to find her hidden treasure.

He traced the outline of the thin strip of soaking wet fabric with his finger, the only thing preventing his entrance to her place of ecstasy. She writhed and moaned softly under his sensual assault. He was lost in the moment, and he could take all her pleasure that morning in his office.

Breaking free of his kiss, she whimpered again. "Axel?"

"Hmm. You okay?" he asked.

"Yes. No, I mean I want to, but I can't … Yes," she stammered, breathless and strained.

In an abrupt, swift motion, he stepped back and ran his hands through his hair. His face was a contorted mixture of pain, pleasure, confusion and passion.

"Whoa. Whoa. Let's slow this down. I don't want to stop, but I don't want there to be any regrets between us, especially after last night. Obviously, you have mixed feelings. Your body is saying 'yes,' but your heart and mind isn't ready," he said, his coarse words wild and ragged.

In a hushed whisper with her head hung low, she poured out her heart. "When I came looking for you, I only wanted to explain the reason for my reaction last night. I was overcome with emotions that I've never experienced before, emotions that have been dormant inside me for a while."

He nodded his head. "I feel the same way, Kerrigan. I've never had feelings for anyone like I have for you. That's the reason I want to get to know you better, to learn more about you and share myself with you."

Avoiding his eyes, she traced invisible shapes onto her lap with her fingertip. "I don't know how to handle these feelings. This is new to me. I don't understand how someone like you can possibly want someone like me."

He smiled warmly at her. "A man like me would consider himself lucky to have a woman like you at his side. You're beautiful, fun and caring and your intelligence was one of the first things I admired about you." What or who had made her insecure?

"Our lives are on opposite ends of two entirely different spectrums." Trembling, she wrapped her arms around herself.

He frowned. "I think we have more in common than either of us realized. We're not that different, and we're the same in every way that matters between a man and a woman."

"You make me lose control, I forget myself and that makes me afraid. I've never lost control of myself with anyone before." He watched the changing expressions on her beautiful face.

His pulse raced. "I like that you lose control with me, but I won't have you unless you trust me with your heart," he said, shaking his head.

"I don't want to be hurt, and you could do that to me easily." Her voice cracked.

"If I only wanted a quick score, there are plenty of eager women out there. I will tell you as many times as I have to until you understand and believe me—I want you, Kerrigan, only you."

He moved closer, careful not to touch her or that would send him over the edge. He had to maintain control in this situation. He loved that she shared this much of herself with him. He took a seat on one of the guest chairs facing Kerrigan who still sat on the desk's edge.

He was trying hard to say the right things to allay her fears and gain her trust.

Her hands folded in her lap, she glanced up, and he held her gaze. "I can't be the first woman you've had strong emotions for. When was your last relationship?"

The memory was too painful. He breathed in deeply and sighed. "It was years ago. It's been an awful long time. What about you? When was your last relationship?" he asked, his head cocked to one side.

She folded her arms across her chest. "I've never had one," she said timidly.

His head jerked up. "What! Why haven't you been in a relationship before?"

"I mean, I've dated here and there, and some guys have tried, but I've never been interested. Not until now." She fidgeted with her hands.

"Well, I'm glad you've had a change of heart." Then a thought occurred to him. Narrowing his eyes, his forehead wrinkled and brows pinched. "I'm a modern man and I know women have needs too. You don't strike me as the type of woman who does the casual sex thing. What do you do for intimacy?"

She shifted on top of the desk, her legs swung and she diverted her gaze. "No, I don't do casual sex. My experiences have been … well, somewhat limited until very recently." Her cheeks glowed crimson, revealing her embarrassment.

His face turned to stone. "How recently, Kerrigan?" His jaw clenched.

"This-weekend-recently," she said, softly.

Like a heat-seeking missile, his gaze landed on her. "What! Are you telling me that you've never had sex, never made out before? You're a virgin?"

Her eyes cast down, she fidgeted with her hands. "You say that like being a virgin is a curse. No, I've never had sex before. What just happened is the farthest I've ever gone."

He tilted his head back until it rested against the back of the chair. Remaining silent for several moments, he brought his head down. She wiggled restlessly were she sat. He knew she was uneasy.

"Axel, what are you thinking? Is this a deal-breaker for you?" Clutching her sides, her voice pitched as if she had ingested a canister of helium.

He released a low chuckle. His response was serious and strained. "No, this isn't a deal-breaker."

She stretched her brow. "But?" she asked nervously.

Axel was furious. He shook his head and then stilled his movements. "Kerrigan, did you have any idea what would have happened if I hadn't stopped last night or a few minutes ago? Were you going to tell me that you were a virgin after I fucked you?" A twinge of pain hit him in the stomach. "Your first time should be unforgettable, only when the time is right. Were you going to give yourself to me right here on my desk?"

She swallowed hard. "I, I don't know. I didn't plan for this to happen. This is all new to me. I was lost in the moment, and well, I was ready, okay." Closing her eyes, she sighed. "I'm not a child, don't I get a say?"

The inflection in his voice rose as his patience dwindled. "You're not ready and no, you don't get a say! What kind of man do you think I am? I'll decide when we're both ready."

He hadn't meant to scare her with his reaction, but he didn't know how to explain why he had reacted so badly to her news. He watched her intently as she trembled at his words.

Eyes blinking fast and darting, her lips curved down. "Are you upset with me because I'm a virgin? I'm sorry."

He softened his tone. "Of course I'm not upset with you for being a virgin. I'm upset about what I almost did without knowing. Kerrigan, last night you were in tears at the thought of me getting too close, too quickly." Slowly lifting his head, he brought his eyes to hers." You're not ready. I won't touch you until you are. I certainly won't let your first time be on a desk in my study."

Tiny wrinkles appeared across her forehead as she frowned. "I didn't know this would upset you so much. Axel, I'm sorry. I thought you wanted this."

He lowered his face into his hand, grabbing his forehead. "Kerrigan, I do want this, I want you, but I had no idea. You can't give yourself to me just because you think that's what I want. Virginity isn't the kind of thing you spring on a guy after the fact. You're not ready. Go get your things and let's go."

Her shoulders slumped. "Aren't we spending the day together?" Slowly, she turned away.

Seeing her hurt and confused expression, he inhaled, closed his eyes and shook his head. "I don't know."

CHAPTER THIRTEEN

She never thought Axel would reject her for being a virgin. She was humiliated. Obviously she'd never felt like a whore before, but feeling like a hard-up virgin slut was probably a close second.

"I'll go get my things." The sting of rejection burned in her throat, and her voice cracked.

Almost in tears again for the second time in less than twenty-four hours, she spun around and ran as fast as she could move her legs to the guest room, her legs quaking beneath her. She slammed the door behind her and locked it, then slumped to the floor beside the bed. Her tears flowed freely down her face as she clung to herself, and shuddered and shook uncontrollably. In less than a week, she had managed to screw up her first chance at a real relationship with a man she found irresistible. He didn't want some inexperienced little girl. He wanted a woman. She gathered her few belongings and placed them on a chair next to the bed.

After washing her face to remove the evidence of her tears, she resolved to forget the last two days. She had been stupid to think she could have a future with a man like him. He was out of her league. Better to end this now before things went too far. If she felt this badly after mere weeks, she could only imagine her heartbreak if she had gotten more deeply involved and he broke up off with her later. She would put on her proverbial mask and go back to pretending everything was normal—he was her boss, she was his employee. Their few moments of indiscretion could be swept under the rug. Nothing unforgivable had happened between them.

***

Shit! He pounded his fist hard on the desk's surface after she left. He was pissed with Kerrigan for not telling him that she was a virgin when he could have easily had his way with her. He was upset the most about how he had handled the situation. He had pushed her away, and he was sure he had seen tears in her eyes before she ran off. This was the very sort of thing that had led him to the notion of no-strings-attached sex as the best choice for him.

He had three options as he saw it. Option one—he could let her go, forget everything that had happened between them and let things go back to the way they were. Option two—he could offer her a healthy severance agreement, get rid of her and forget she existed. Option three—he could be honest, confront his past and move forward with the woman who had seized his every thought, invaded his senses, captured his heart and made him feel as if there were hope for love to blossom. After serious internal debate, he stood and made his way to the door. The only choice that could be made was the one that inflicted the least pain on Kerrigan.

He tried twisting the knob, but the door was locked.

"I'll be right out."

Kerrigan's shaky and unsteady voice forced a twinge of pain through his chest. The last thing he ever wanted to do was to hurt her. "Kerrigan, may I please come in?" His tone was tender and calm. He was about to do the hardest thing he'd ever have to do.

"Here I am. I'm ready." The door flung open, and there she was with all her things in hand. The sheen in her eyes gave her away. She had been crying.

His voice was low and husky, his face riddled with remorse. "I really don't want you to leave yet. I owe you an apology and an explanation."

"It's okay, Axel. It's probably for the best. Let's just stop this now before things get out of hand. We will never work out. I've been caught up in my emotions. I'm not thinking with my head. Let's go back to the way things were before … all this," she said, gesturing with her arms waving between them. "Let's forget the past few weeks."

"Kerrigan, what's happening between us has been going on a helluva lot longer than a few weeks, and I don't want to forget a single minute. Everything I said is true. I want you, only you. I want to know everything about you. What happened in my office brought some painful memories back from a long time ago."

She shifted from one foot to the next, looking pass him to avoid his face. "Let's just keep things professional between us. I'm no good at this relationship stuff."

He was going to break through to her again. Cupping her delicate face with his large hands, he stared into her eyes. "No, I won't go back to the way things were before. There's something so powerful between us, I couldn't ignore my feelings if I tried. I was a jerk. Will you at least give me a chance to explain?"

The way she leaned into his touch, he knew the icy cage that held her emotions captive was melting away.

"Okay. Explain." Her tone was stern, but he was glad for the opportunity.

"There's something I need to show you. Will you come with me?"

He held out his hand to her, and she accepted. His pace slow, deliberately enjoying the feel of her hand in his and delaying what was to come. They walked in silence with their fingers intermingled until he led them back to his office.

Axel released her hand and pointed to the large leather sofa opposite the front of his oak desk. "Will you sit there while I look for something?" He dug through a wooden file cabinet and retrieved a thick gray file folder, and then made his way to the sofa where she sat. He sat in the chair next to the sofa, avoiding proximity to her and the electricity between them that made them both rage out of control.

Axel searched the folder until he found a stack of worn and yellowed newspaper clippings. He held one in his hand and stared at the clipping, the article had resurrected pain, angering him to the point that fire behind his eyes nearly scorched the paper.

Sucking in a deep breath, he handed the clipping to Kerrigan without looking at her. "What I'm about to share with you is my darkest secret and biggest source of pain." His chest pounded. "I've never shared this with anyone except close family members. Read, then ask any questions you'd like."

He knew this was either the end or the beginning of whatever would be between them. His gut ached as if he had gone five rounds against the heavy weight champ.

After reading the article, she slowly lifted her bewildered eyes, searching his. "Oh my god!" He cringed at the terror in her eyes. Did she think he was a monster?

Her glassy glare sent a chill up his spine. "Did you do this, Axel?" Her voice teetered on the edge of tears.

Lowering his head, his chin pressed into his chest. "No, Kerrigan, I didn't," he muttered through gritted teeth.

His heart sank. Reaching out to her, "Read these too," he said, handing her three more articles.

After reading them all, she inhaled and blew out a hard breath. "When did this happen?"

His shoulders sagged. "About twelve years ago. I spent almost two years of my life in courtroom battles fighting the rape allegation against Sara Murphy before being exonerated. If it weren't for the email exchanges between Sara and her two roommates exposing their extortion plot, I'd be locked up or worse."

"What happened exactly?" she asked, her shrunken voice constricted and husky.

He turned his head. He didn't want her to see him like this—filled with anger, rage and fear. He closed his eyes. "Sara's friends confessed after entering into a plea deal, and the case was eventually dismissed."

"How did you get through this?"

The pang in his chest forced his eyes open. Her words weren't accusatory. "I'm still working on it. My pride and reputation was destroyed. I lost all faith and trust in women to the point that I objectified them. I'm not proud of that."

She looked up at Axel with sympathy. "Axel, I'm…I didn't know. I'm sorry."

He didn't want her pity. He turned his eyes away, glaring at the base of the desk. "Sara and I had been going out for six months. I really liked her. We were young, and I thought I was in love. She told me she was a virgin. I told her I'd wait until she was ready." Narrowed eyes and clenched jaw, he paused. Waves of anger rolled through his gut. "We were in her dorm room the night she decided she was ready. We had sex. She didn't behave like a virgin in the bed. Immediately afterwards, she started crying and screaming, asking me why I raped her. I was so confused. I thought I hurt her."

He shook his head, a knot formed in his dry throat. "I didn't know what was going on. I certainly didn't think I was being set up. Seconds later, one of her roommates walked into the room, and then the other." Kerrigan stood and moved closer to him, sitting on the arm of the leather sofa. "They attacked and beat the crap out of me, called the police and said they'd witnessed me attack Sara. That was the worst two years of my life."

She sat motionless, gazing at him with her big hazel eyes. He had revealed his most painful secret, the thing that he had never shared with anyone else, yet he felt compelled to tell her, to open himself up to her completely. He knew what was at risk, but she needed to know his past, even if that meant losing her.

He turned and stared into her eyes. This was his silent plea. "I lost focus on school. My relationship with my parents was strained. It was hell." He paused. "I know I can be aggressive, but Kerrigan, I didn't rape her." Desperation oozed from his every pore.

His heart raced. With tightened shoulders, he drew his elbows into his sides and clutched the folder hard until his knuckles turned stark white. He had never felt more afraid and exposed than now.

***

Kerrigan was stunned. "Axel, I don't know what to say."

Slumping over, he exhaled a hard breath, and then stared blankly into the middle of the room. "I understand, Kerrigan. I do."

"Well, I don't understand. I don't understand how anyone could be that heartless and evil toward you." Betrayed by someone that he cared about must have been torturous.

He jerked his head up, his eyes flashing bright, met hers. "You believe me? You're not going to walk away?"

She heard his vulnerability and saw his anguish. "Yes, of course I believe you. I know you well enough to know you couldn't do something like that." Thinking about what could have happened to him if the truth hadn't been discovered made her sick, the pangs gripping Kerrigan's insides and nausea rising.

He was just as torn as she was with the desire to move forward but too afraid to trust himself or anyone else. She reached out to touch his shoulder, but he flinched, caught her hand and stared into her eyes. She wanted to offer him some reassurance that her feelings for him were genuine and unchanged. It would take time. He wasn't ready either. He had to learn to trust her too.

Sliding her hand from his, she lowered her gaze. "I'm so sorry, Axel, about before … about today. You're right. We're not ready. I can imagine trusting anyone must be difficult, after what she did to you, but I'm not like her."

He jerked his head back, his eyes widened and the corner of his mouth lifted. "Kerrigan, you're an amazing woman. I tell you I was accused of raping someone and you think *I* don't trust *you*." His tender eyes peered longingly at her. "I know you're nothing like Sara. I would never compare you to her." He reached out, wrapped his fingers around the hand that he had pushed away and held her hand in his. "I can't believe there isn't a part of you that doesn't believe me. I've lost good friends who believed I had gotten away with rape because of my family's wealth and my father's reach into the judicial system."

Kerrigan tilted her head slightly, drawing her lips into a faint smile. "Axel, those so-called friends you lost weren't really true friends. True friends wouldn't have turned against you. I know you could never do something like that."

There was no doubt in Kerrigan's mind that Axel was innocent. A heavy heart pained her, realizing that he hadn't been able to move on, but also proud. He hadn't let the lowest point in his life define whom he would become.

"Sara missed out on what could have been a great thing. Look at you now. You run your own successful agency, made a name for yourself in the ad world despite her attempt to destroy you and you're okay to look at, too," she teased, hoping to lighten the mood.

He gave his slow sexy smirk. "Miss Mulls, was that a compliment? It sounds like you might actually like me, and maybe even trust me a little."

"I guess that did sound that way, huh?" she said, the edges of her mouth creasing.

"Finding out you're a virgin brought old memories to life. I haven't been in a serious relationship because of this, and I want a real chance with you, Kerrigan. We need to take things slowly, despite what our bodies seem to want. What do you say?"

"Slow is good." She smiled back.

He raised his brow. "That means no more making out," he said, laying down the law as if he were trying to convince himself as he said the words aloud.

"Okay, easy." She nodded.

"Easy for who? Maybe for you," he said gruffly under his breath, making her laugh.

He nodded his head. "Get to know each other with no pressure."

She knew he needed this as much as she did. He needed to learn to trust again. He needed time to heal.

"I'm game," she said.

"Come on. Why don't I give you a tour of the house, and then we can go out and get some fresh air?"

Kerrigan smiled. "Sounds perfect," she said, feeling more hopeful after their talk.

He had shown her a side of himself that she had never expected. At work, he was all business. With her, he was the aggressive, dominant male in hot pursuit, and the vulnerable, genuine man who needed rescuing. She liked the many sides of Axel. She was looking forward to spending time with him with no pressure and just getting to know him better.

***

They rode in silence, listening to the vibes of Mikky Ekko's Pull Me Down track flowing through the speakers—Axel's secret anthem to her. He reached over, grabbed Kerrigan's hand in his for a few moments, and let go. She glanced at him and flashed a bright smile.

His eyes fixed to the road, he broke their silent reverie. "Do you know what I love about you?" He surprised himself. His heart raced, and he blinked hard twice. *Oh, shit!* He hadn't meant to use the word love, but it slipped out.

She wrinkled her brow. "I've been trying to figure that out," she teased. She hadn't been fazed by the word. *Good!*

"The way your entire face lights up when you smile. You are a natural beauty—flawless mocha skin, full lips, beautiful hazel eyes. I could go on and on."

"Axel, you're making me blush."

"Hold your blush to the end, please. I'm not done." He smiled. "You have a kind and caring heart, and I admire your hard work. You have a brilliant mind and a great personality. You're witty, and I enjoy your company. I shared my darkest secret with you and you never even flinched. You're an amazing woman, Kerrigan Mulls." He paused and caught her large innocent eyes staring up at him. "Okay, commence with your blushing."

She covered her face with her hands and shook her head. "Thank you." Glancing back at him, "Do you know what I like about you?"

"Nope. Don't want to know," he said. "I'm taking you out, and this is day is all about you, not me. When you take me out, then you can tell me all the wonderful things you like about me."

Pinching her eyebrows together in surprise, "Are you serious?" she asked.

"Yep."

She laughed harder now.

"This way, you'll have to go out with me again," he teased.

"Okay, can I at least ask you a question?"

"Anything you want baby. I'm an open book." He leaned over and squeezed her knee.

"Have you ever dated outside your race before?" She blurted out.

He shot her a curious look. "You mean outside the human race?" he questioned, giving her a smug grin. "No, I've never dated outside of the human race. Cows, goats and other live stock aren't my thing." Laughing again, she rolled her eyes. "Kerrigan, does the fact that I'm white bother you?"

"No, race doesn't matter to me. Most white men I know aren't into black women or at least won't act on their attraction."

He looked over at her again. "If that's true, then it's a good thing for me that I'm not like most white men you know." He was relieved that race wasn't an issue.

"It's a good thing for me too," she said, grinning as wide as rush hour traffic in Atlanta is grueling.

He kept down the volume so they could continue their conversation.

"Tell me about your family. Where did you grow up?" he asked.

The sun beamed brightly into the passenger side of the vehicle, and Kerrigan lowered the sun visor. Squinting, she looked over at him. "Well, I grew up in San Diego. Mom and Dad are fantastic. They taught my brother Jordan and I the value and importance of hard work, and respect for others and self. We went to church most Sundays and volunteered every month. Pretty average stuff, I suppose."

"Not average. Sounds as if you had a wholesome upbringing. So, what about your parents and brother?"

Picking up her handbag, she retrieved a pair of sunglasses and slid them on. "Well, my brother is a cardiovascular surgeon. He lives in San Diego with his wife Nicole and their twin girls Kara and Mira. Both my parents are semi-retired. Mom was a teacher and dad retired from the Army. He was a police officer until he was injured in an accident some years ago. He works part-time for the police department, but does 'desk work' as he calls it. Mom tutors kids and teaches piano lessons. That's about it really. What about your family?"

He kept his eyes on the road and hands on the steering wheel. "Well, Miss Mulls, I didn't have such a wholesome upbringing. We lived in lots of different places for my father's job—Boston, Manhattan, Chicago and Dallas. I'm sure I'm forgetting some of the places where we lived. We moved so often, I lost track."

"Does your mother still work or is she retired?" she asked.

"My mother has never worked a day in her life. She's a full-time socialite, hosting or attending parties, galas and fundraisers or engaging in the latest gossip."

She relaxed her head against the seat. "And your father is an attorney. Does he still practice?"

Giving her a sidelong glance, "Yes. He traveled most of my childhood and was never around. I didn't get to know him until

I was much older. Ryker, my kid brother, followed my father's footsteps. I went into business."

She faced him and tilted her head up, brows pressed inward. "That doesn't sound too bad. You said you didn't have a wholesome childhood. Why?"

Inhaling a deep breath, he released it with a long sigh. "My mother and father were too busy with their own lives to instill altruistic values in my brother and me. We didn't always do things together, the way normal families do I suppose. Things are much better now that we don't share a roof. We speak once every few weeks or so, and I see them a couple of times a year, sometimes more."

"Are you close with your brother?" she asked.

He maneuvered the vehicle from one lane to another, steering clear of a sputtering yellow van straight out of 1970. "Yeah, we hang out sometimes. You'll get to meet him one day." Lane change safely complete, he glanced at her. "Your mom teaches piano lessons. Do you play?"

"I used to. My apartment is too small for a piano. I love it, but I'm out of practice. Do you play an instrument or have any talents?"

"I don't play the piano, although I do have one. You'll have to come over and play for me sometime." Pausing, he narrowed his eyes. "I do have other talents that I'm eager to share with you. You'll have to wait a while before you enjoy those though," he said, and then bit his bottom lip, waiting for her reaction.

She blushed and squirmed in her seat. "Exactly to what talents are you referring Mr. Christensen? If I have to wait, I'd like to know it's worth it."

Boldly, she ran the tip of her long delicate finger down his arm sending an exhilarating shiver through his body. "Mmm." He released a low groan. "Don't tempt me Miss Mulls. You don't want to throw stones at this giant. I'll turn this vehicle around and violate every damn rule we agreed to earlier today."

"I didn't know you were a man so easily torn from your convictions."

Looking down at his lap, he eyed his hard-on and her gaze followed. "Only when it comes to you," he said, flashing a wicked smile.

The vehicle pulled into a crowded parking lot. He hadn't told her where he was taking her that afternoon, keeping her in suspense. Jumping out of the SUV, he opened her door and extended his hand offering to help her down. They made their way toward a large white brick building. There was no signage anywhere to be found.

"I hope you enjoy mountain biking."

"It's been a while, but yes I do."

"Good. We're picking up our rental bikes here."

"What would you have done if I said I couldn't ride?" she asked.

The corner of his mouth lifted into a slow, sexy smirk. Leaning in close, he whispered. "I would have said it's another thing I get to teach you to ride."

***

When they walked into the building, he immediately spotted Betty, who made her way to them and threw her pale arms around Axel's neck, giving him a firm hug. He wrapped his arms around her warmly, greeting her with equal enthusiasm.

"It's been such a long time. How have you been? Is this Kerrigan" She paused. "Oh, Axel, she's gorgeous." Not giving him a chance to answer her questions, the white-haired woman looked at Kerrigan. "Every time I talk to him, he goes on and on about you. It's such a pleasure to meet the woman who finally has captured Axel's heart. I'm Betty." She pulled Kerrigan into her arms and squeezed tightly.

"Oh?" Kerrigan answered with a questioning smile, flashing him a skeptical look over Betty's shoulder. "Nice to meet you too … Betty."

"The bikes are ready and everything…"

"Okay!" Startled by the loud thunder of his voice interrupting her mid-speech, Betty jumped. "Thanks for your help Betty. We'd better get going." He liked Betty, and she was a dear friend of his family's, but the woman talked too much.

"Oh, right! Let's go get your bikes." They headed to the restrooms, which were located on the outside of the building, to change their clothes. He had packed riding gear for them both. He came out first, strapped on his helmet and then sat on a bench and waited for Kerrigan. When she finally appeared, he stopped breathing. Her shorts highlighted her shapely golden brown legs, and he struggled to stop gawking. The fitted shirt accentuated the delicate curves of her small frame and voluptuous breasts. Her long hair flowed down her back underneath her helmet. As she got closer, his pants tightened around his groin. *How in the hell am I going to keep my hands off her?*

"I'm ready," she announced.

"I need a few minutes," he said gruffly.

"Is everything all right?" Her forehead wrinkled with worry.

"Yeah, just give me a minute," he said flatly and then cleared his throat.

She noticed the hulking bulge in his lap. "Oh … Oh! I'm sorry," She turned beet red and laughed at the same time.

"Woman, do you see what you're doing to me? You're driving me crazy."

"I'm sorry. Is there anything I can do?" Her expression was serious as she moved closer to touch his shoulder, but then stopped.

"I can think of a few things," he gave her a dangerous grin. *Spend the night with me and never leave.*

"I'm sure you can, but I think what you have in mind might violate our agreement."

"What I have in mind would most definitely violate our agreement." He took a deep breath and exhaled. "Let's go." He stood up and bit his bottom lip. His body had never responded so spontaneously to any woman the way it did to hers. Despite his best intentions to go slowly with her, he didn't know if he'd be strong enough to wait much longer before fully claiming her.

They rode side by side down the bike trail laughing and talking.

He slowed his speed and turned toward her, peering at her from underneath his green and black helmet. "What kind of music do you like?" he asked.

"I like a little of everything from pop and rock to alternative and jazz. Nineties throwbacks are also great. What about you?"

"I like a little bit of everything too, but classic R&B and old school hip hop are at the top of my list."

Her lips curled down into a frown. "Really?" she asked.

"Why does that surprise you? I bet I could teach you a thing or two."

Rolling her eyes at him, she smirked. "You'll have to add it to your growing list of things to teach me."

"I'll be sure to do that because you'll need a healthy appreciation for classic R&B to enhance the experience of the number one thing on my list." Her eyes widened and her mouth fell open. He chuckled. "But only when we're both ready," he added.

The corners of his lips dipped, his gaze scanning the asphalt trail as they rode. "I have a confession. You should know about some of my quarks." He knew this would spark her interest.

"Everyone has a thing. I have several, and I hope you don't hold them against me. You tell me yours, and I'll tell you mine." She smiled.

Focused on the trail, he saw the split. "Follow me."

"Where are we going?"

"No questions. Just follow me. This way." Hanging a left, he led them down a secluded bike trail surrounded by wild flowers and tall evergreens. "Okay. I have this weird thing about not letting my bare feet touch the ground." He hoped she had a good sense of humor. "You'll always find me in a pair of socks. There are only two places where I make an exception, in bed and on the beach."

She shook her head. "That's not too bad. I have to close my bathroom door when I brush my teeth. I don't know why, but I shut the bathroom door in my apartment, and I'm the only one there."

He pursed his lips and nodded his head. "I'm always aroused by you and I can't stop staring. You're beautiful. It's becoming a thing," he admitted.

Kerrigan threw her head back, her laughter boomeranging in echo. "I may have noticed," she said, and continued laughing. "Well, I can't sleep without hugging my pillow," she said. "I know it's weird."

"Really? Sounds as if you're missing something."

Her laugh subsided into quiet. "I've done it for as long as I can remember," she said, shaking her head.

"I think your pillow is a surrogate for the man you need who'll give you what your heart deserves, cherish your body tenderly and sensually, and keep you safe in his arms. I'll take replacing your pillow as a personal challenge."

Her breath seized, gaping at him with wide, timid eyes.

"Someday, Kerrigan, I promise I'll make sure you don't need that pillow ever again." He knew from her expression that he hit the right chord. "You should know that I'm a man of my word."

They continued riding for five minutes until she broke the tension-filled silence.

"Giving back to the community is important. I volunteer twice a month at a couple of elementary schools reading to first and second graders. How do you give back?"

"I give with my wallet and thanks to you I've significantly increased my donations this year."

"There are so many people who need help. Donations are great, but your time is invaluable. I know you're busy, but you should consider giving some of your time. I also mentor and tutor middle school students once a month. There's nothing like seeing their faces when the light clicks on, and they learn something they've been struggling to understand. Maybe…"

Finishing her sentence, "Maybe we could go together sometime."

"Yes. I think you would find the experience rewarding."

"You like helping kids, don't you?" he asked.

She nodded her head. "I love it. Some of the kids I help don't get any encouragement or support at home. It makes me feel good to help them with their school work or personal issues."

"You're giving and compassionate, and you love kids. I love that about you. Do you want a large family of your own someday?"

She kept her eyes fixed ahead down the long winding trail. "Well, I hope to have at least a couple of kids one day, I suppose."

"You don't sound too sure," he said, glancing at her.

She sighed. "Ideally, I'd like to settle down first, but life is unpredictable. Who knows what the future holds."

"Ah, I see." He smiled. "I don't think you have much to worry about. I'd say chances are in your favor that you'll settle down and have a family of your own someday."

"What about you? Do you want a big family?" she asked.

"I want whatever my future wife wants," he replied, giving her a coy smile. She didn't seem to catch on to his subtle hint.

She frowned. "Really? If your wife wanted ten kids or if she didn't want children at all, would you just go along with her demands? That's a noble gesture, but Axel, surely what you want matters too," she scolded.

"Well baby, my preference is two children, but if you wanted more, then we could have more. I hope you don't want an army, though." This time he held her timid gaze, waiting for her response.

She choked a nervous laugh back, her eyes moistening. "You, you can't possibly think of me in this way. Me?" Her voice was shaky.

"You. You're the only woman I've ever thought about in this way." His reply was short and pointed. "How does that make you feel?"

She hesitated for a moment before responding, wrinkles creasing her brow. "Makes me nervous, but in a good way."

"Makes me nervous in a good way too." He gave her a Cheshire cat-on-steroids grin, his pulse racing.

CHAPTER FOURTEEN

When they reached Axel's secret destination, they parked and locked up their bikes at a nearby rack. He took her by the hand and led her down a winding trail that descended into a valley flanked by large grass-covered hills looming all around them. At the base of the valley was a wide creek with wild flowers growing along its banks. Tall willowy trees and jagged rocks lined its edges. Streams of water cascading over steep slopes created a series of beautiful waterfalls that flowed into the water.

Kerrigan gasped. "Wow, this is absolutely beautiful!"

His eyes affixed to her. "Yes she is."

His remark wasn't lost on her. Her cheeks tinted like red roses in bloom. He always found a way to turn up the heat. *Don't get caught up. He's only flattering you. This is just infatuation, and he'll be moving on to someone new in no time.*

They walked hand-in-hand, his large masculine hand wrapped around her delicate, soft one until they reached a large shade tree covered in vibrant shades of green. The sound of the tree's leaves rustling in the wind was reminiscent of light raindrops falling. She stopped. Closing her eyes, she delighted in the sound washing over her in waves.

"You like that," he said, words spoken softly. "The tranquility, the breeze."

She opened her eyes and grinned broadly. "I love the sound of rain falling. The leaves, they sound just like rain. This is … unbelievable."

Releasing her hand, he brought his palm to her face and caressed her cheek tenderly with his hand. "I love to see you so relaxed, so carefree..." Staring at her as if he ran out of words, he paused. She had never seen that look in his eyes before, a new emotion that she couldn't place. "…so beautiful." His voice was a whisper.

Beneath the tree laid a large blanket where a picnic spread was set out. A bottle of Riesling, wine glasses and unlit candles were set on top of a picnic basket. Her heart hammered against her breast and her legs trembled under her quivering body. This was the most romantic and beautiful place she had ever been, not to mention the fact that she couldn't keep her eyes off him. She leaned her head against his shoulder, relishing the feel of him. His arm swathed her pulling her closer to him. Knowing that he had especially arranged the day just for her, she barely contained her emotions. *He probably does this for all of his dates. You're not special.* The thought was sobering, snatching her back into reality. She had to keep her guard up.

"What do you think?" His brow wrinkled and head tilted down, he studied her face with his intense narrow gaze. As if he were directly addressing her unspoken thoughts, he added, "I hope you like my surprise. I've never done anything like this before. We have the entire area to ourselves. Let's sit down."

Tears pooled in her eyes. "Your surprise is perfect, Axel. I … I can't believe you did this. You did this for me. No one has ever done anything romantic for me before. This place is so beautiful," she said, her voice shaky, choking back tears.

His eyes sparkled. "You inspire me, Kerrigan. I think I'd do anything for you."

Conflicted, she was afraid to hope for a future with him. Wasn't she merely a conquest to him? Once he captured her … well, despite what she thought, she would enjoy this day.

He offered his hand and helped her down onto the blanket.

"Close your eyes and open your mouth," he said, a twinkle in his eyes. "You can trust me, baby."

She wanted him to press his lips to hers so badly that she ached to the core.

She closed her eyes then opened wide and awaited his next move. She heard the creaking sound of the basket opening. The sour sweetness melted onto her taste buds. "Mmm. That is delicious. What is this?"

He moved in close and whispered in her ear. "Concord grapes. Glad you like them. I hand-picked them for you."

If he had asked, she would have let him make love to her right there in broad daylight, under the tree and on that picnic blanket. He didn't ask.

They fed each other an assortment of treats from the basket, tempting and teasing and satisfying their physical hunger. Kerrigan had never liked the company of a man more than this date. For the first time since she stepped foot in his office more than a year ago, she was relaxed, enjoying him, her armor surrendered and her heart exposed.

"Lie down on your stomach. You've made this day so special for me, this is the least I can do."

"Yes ma'am. I like the sound of that. How can I resist?" Lying down, he placed his head down on the blanket, closed his eyes and smiled.

She swiped playfully at his arm. “I hope I don’t disappoint you.”

He let out a throaty laugh. “Miss Mulls, you never disappoint me.”

She grabbed hold of his shoulders and gripped him hard. “This is something I learned while paying my way through school.” She rubbed and pulled, digging her fingers into his firm, muscular shoulders, massaging deep.

“Oh, god. Kerrigan.” He moaned. “Your hands are magic.”

She smiled. “So I’ve been told.”

He poked his head up again. “I’m jealous. Who else have you given this massage to? No past boyfriends I hope.”

“I’ve never had a boyfriend.”

As if that were his cue, he rolled over and placed his hands behind his head. “I still can’t believe you’ve never … never even had a boyfriend.”

“The longest time I dated anyone, was two months, but he wasn’t my boyfriend.”

He leaned up, placing his weight on his forearms. “That’s close enough. What was the reason the relationship didn’t work?”

“I dated this guy named Greg for two months. I liked him, but he was a complete jerk. He told me that I was too beautiful to be taken seriously and too smart for a man to stick around.” Her chest tightened, and her throat turned dry. The pain of his words still stung her heart. “He dumped me when I refused to have sex with him.” She’d never even told Ashley the details. She gazed down at him, inhaled a breath and sighed.

Axel sat up straight, frowning. “I’m sorry, Kerrigan. He sounds like a colossal asshole to me.” His hand placed under her chin, he raised her downturned face up to him.

"After similar dating experiences, I just became fed up. That's why I don't date anymore." She blinked repeatedly.

Always attuned to her emotional needs even without her saying a word, he stood and held out his hand. "Then, to be given this chance, I am privileged." His slow sexy smile melted her heart. "Let's go for a walk."

An hour later, they settled along the creek's edge, resting on the bank. She was enamored with the scenery. He pulled her close to him and she nestled her head against his chest.

"I'll wait as long as I have to, Kerrigan," he made love to her with his sweet and gentle words. "You're beautiful, kind, smart and fun. Everything this man could want," complimenting her. "Plus you can't keep your hands off me," teasing her and tantalizing her senses to the limit.

Despite her best effort, denying her feelings had been difficult. "I've never felt about anyone the way I feel about you." She admitted, lost in the moment with Axel.

He tightened his grip around her waist and whispered softly, "Kerrigan, I'm not interested in a short-term fling. I want more than that with you."

Glancing up, she met his tender gaze. "Slow, right?"

His eyes blazed with passion. "Yes, slow," he said while his right hand teased her arm, dancing up and down, radiating tingles up her spine.

They had enjoyed each other's company in the private haven that Axel created for them, and he hadn't even tried to kiss her once. Dusk was beginning to fall now, and they decided to walk back to the picnic blanket under the tree. When they returned, he lit the candles and carefully placed them on the sturdy base of the picnic basket. Sitting across from her, he twisted his restless hands together.

Fidgeting, he rubbed the palms of his hands on his shorts. With eyes wide and bright, he licked his lips incessantly and kept clearing his throat. Something was different between them—a new nervous energy so charged that she was about to ignite.

Axel poured two glasses of wine and handed one to Kerrigan. "For you."

Avoiding his gaze, she reached out and accepted the glass. "Thank you," her response was spoken softly from trembling lips. At the graze of his fingertips against her hand, anxiety rolled through her insides in waves and the glass tumbled over, white wine soaking her.

He grabbed a paper towel and reached over. "Here, let me help." Blotting her naked thighs, he moved up to her shirt, pressing the towel into her breasts.

"Thank you." The words came out raspy. His shaky hands continued patting her until she backed away.

He said he wanted to make her first time with him the most memorable and spectacular experience of her life. One part of her wanted nothing more than for him to claim her on the earth where they sat. Another part of her was terrified of him getting too close for fear he would break her heart. Keeping her distance, she avoided his eyes and kept her head down.

Here, she was in the most romantic place she'd ever been, with the handsomest guy she'd ever known, having experienced sensations she'd never felt before and on the brink of falling so deep that she couldn't image how she'd ever recover when Axel broke her heart.

***

The setting was beautiful, nearly perfect, but too soon to do what he really wanted. After all, they made an agreement. He had to keep reminding himself that only weeks had passed, although he felt like he knew her a lifetime. Together they were easy, and the relationship felt right. *Ask her to marry you.* The thought surprised him, but he didn't turn away from the idea. He had always been in touch with his feelings, never shying away or denying them. He knew the moment he laid eyes on her that he wanted Kerrigan Mulls. She was his future. Now to convince her.

***

They both lay on their backs looking up into the early evening sky. He shifted, then reared up so that he lay on his side, chin in palm, hovering over her. He stared deeply into her hazel eyes. The sensation started in her feet, moved up to her hammering heart, tingling and warm, flowing through her like a tidal wave crashing onto the shore. The trees, the ground, the sky all disappeared, and they were floating, soaring, whirling, hopelessly lost in each other.

He leaned in close. "Kerrigan, I'm serious about my intentions toward you. The more I get to know you, the more serious I'm becoming. I want to woo you in the good old-fashioned sense."

Her mouth fell open and she stopped breathing.

"I want you head over heels so that you'll never say 'no' to anything I ask of you."

He moved closer, lowered his head and covered her lips in heated fusion. Their tongues collided and thrashed in a fit of passionate fury. Axel slipped his large hand under the clingy spandex shirt, and anxious fingers crawled slowly across Kerrigan's flesh inching toward the cover of her lace cami bra. Her body trembled, and his gaze met Kerrigan's approving eyes. Long fingers wiggled under the stretchy lace, lifted the sheer fabric away and caressed a freed bosom. A guttural groan, the release of pinned up emotion, escaped his lips. Swiftly, he mounted her, opened her to accept his girth, his burly frame nested between her thighs. His cock was a steel rod pressed hard against her sex, an exhilarating first.

Their lips ripped apart as he lifted her shirt and captured a caramel nipple in his mouth. He sucked gently, circling it with his swirling tongue. He continued his sweet torture edging her to the point of no return. She cried out, the rogue sound escaped her lips without harness. He moaned against her tender flesh, the vibration forcing another whimper from her soul. Perched above her on his arms, he pried his lips from her swollen breasts, burying his face into her neck. Slowly, his lips edged along her jaw line until they seized hers, his tongue thrusting deeply into her mouth. He reared up, their eyes met, tender to teary and wanting to wanted.

He stilled. "Kerrigan, I … I," whispered words stammered into her ear, incoherent, but without the need for explanation.

Breathless, she whispered back, "Yes, Axel. Yes."

Her eyes were shut, and hands gripped Axel's shoulders hard, braced for whatever he was about to do next. So ready to be claimed, her bones rattled in her flesh.

***

Holding Kerrigan's gaze as she lay beneath him, he desired nothing more than to take her and strip her of her virginity right there underneath the open sky, but he was more determined to respect her and win her heart. He wanted to devour her, but instead.

"We need to stop before we go too far," Axel muttered.

Her eyes were still closed as she nodded a wispy "Oh." The only thing she could say.

"Besides, I don't want to end up in headlines. Naked man bucked by deer at a local park."

She blushed. The joke worked, slowly lifting their heavy sedation.

This feeling was new to Axel. His desire to cherish her and connect with her on a deeper level was stronger than his lust, a first. He knew, and maybe she did too, but they were both well on the way to falling head over heels in love. Kerrigan fixed her bra and adjusted her shirt. He captured her eyes before speaking, trying to find the right words. *I love you. Marry me.* His inward thoughts and feelings crowding his consciousness jarred him. He didn't have the courage to say those words. It was too soon. He stood up and reached for her hand, trying to break the intensity.

"Baby, we'd better head back."

"Yes. It'll be very dark soon," she muttered softly.

They rode back to return the bikes, neither one saying much and each deep in thought about what was happening between them, a comfortable, reflective silence. Later, he would explore the emotions that told him she was the woman who would wear his ring.

***

Axel rounded the corner and pulled into the parking deck. Reluctant to let her go, this was the only choice. Things were moving too quickly, but the chemistry and connection between them was remarkable. He knew she felt it too. His Land Rover pulled up next to her small Volkswagen EOS convertible.

Reaching for her hand, he caressed her fingers. His blue eyes darkened with passion. "I really enjoyed the time we spent together. I wish I didn't have to let you go." He paused. "Spend the night ... in the guest bedroom, of course." He knew the danger of his offer.

Kerrigan squirmed in her seat. "I had a nice time too, but I don't think spending the night is wise." Breaking his grip, her hand fell to her lap.

He placed his palm under her chin. "You're right. I have no restraint where you're concerned." The pad of his thumb stroked her bottom lip.

Paralyzed by his touch, she stared up at him helplessly, leaning into his hand. "Besides, we both have other things to do. I have a ton of errands to run tomorrow." Her words uttered mechanically, without thought or inflection.

Hypnotic eyes tormented Axel. "One more thing—I'm not sneaking around at work anymore. I have feelings for you, Kerrigan, and I won't hide what's happening between us. I don't care who knows." Moving closer, he succumbed, utterly entranced. His tender kiss pressed her lips, the sensation lingered and held them together for minutes.

Slowly, she pulled away from his anchor, winded. "Axel, what's happening between us?" Her voice soft, and eyes dazed, and tender, searched his.

He moved his hand to her cheek, gently caressing her. "Well obviously, there's a strong attraction between us. I care for you a great deal. I'd like to think that we're exclusive." Her flawless skin glowed under the dimly cast light. "I know where I see us heading." His gut wrenched as soon as those last words left his mouth. He wasn't ready for this conversation, yet.

Shifting in her seat, she wrapped her arms around herself. "I care for you too." Her forehead wrinkling, she forced a nervous smile. Light from cars passing on the nearby road banded her face. "Where do you see us heading?" Her voice trembled.

"We'll talk about that later. Let's work on keeping the pace slow and steady for now."

***

Eyebrows pressed in, and forehead wrinkled, she pondered. Were they more than friends? If they were exclusive, did that make her his girlfriend? Where did he think they were heading? Could she handle a man like him?

She nodded her head. "Yes, slow and steady."

"Good, then we're agreed." He smirked, his eyes roving her curves. "I can handle slow, but not too slow."

Although she had no idea to what exactly she had agreed, the intentions behind his words and his lusty gaze registered clearly with her. One thing she knew for sure was that he wanted her body, and she wanted to give it to him. This man tempted her good sense.

Backing away from his caress, she changed the subject. "We never talked about McBride. We really do need a plan."

He raised one eyebrow. "Don't worry about McBride, we'll work out a plan in a couple of weeks. He's not going anywhere, and neither am I. I won't let you run away from us."

She flushed. "Well, I guess I'd better get going." Her hand flew to the door handle. "Thank you for a lovely weekend, Axel. Will I see you at some point next week?"

Before she could open the door, he moved closer, preventing her escape. He grabbed her forearm and pulled her to him, securing her lips with his once more. Her head swam and every part of her burned. After a few moments, he pulled back.

"No, we won't see each other next week. I'm the keynote speaker at a marketing conference in New York. I'm glad you had a good time. Check your email while I'm gone."

***

Sunday, September 23

As much as she enjoyed being in Axel's company, Kerrigan was glad to be back at home. Two days felt like an eternity. She settled in, grabbed a quick bite to eat and listened to her voice mail. Mom had called twice, and her brother Jordan had called once. She would call them later. Right now, she needed to talk to Ashley to help her make sense of everything.

She told Ashley everything, except the intimate conversations she and Axel had about his ordeal with Sara.

"He's so into you. You hit the jackpot!" Ashley's excitement seeped through the handset.

Kerrigan leaned against the barren kitchen counter with the phone pressed to her ear. "Ashley, it's not like that. I don't want anything from him. You know me better than that."

"That's not what I meant. I know you're not a gold digger. I meant you landed a fine-ass man who happens to be a gentleman, and it doesn't hurt that the dude is loaded. Jackpot!"

"Yeah, but I'm confused about what it all means. He keeps alluding to us being together in the future. He says we're exclusive. It's all happening so fast. I don't know how to process everything. Is he infatuated and just saying what he's feeling in the moment, telling me what he thinks I want to hear?" She released a sigh, put on the speakerphone and then set the handset down.

"Are you freaking kidding me? Stop analyzing everything and just feel. Axel is talking about having a future with you, talking about kids with you, and you're confused?"

Kerrigan opened bare kitchen cabinets one at a time, taking mental note of needed items. "He can't be serious about me. After two days?" Grimacing, her nose turned upward. She really needed to buy groceries.

"Kerri, you've known the man for more than two days. This thing between you two has been building for months. You've only been intimate with him for two days."

"Do you think he's only trying to get me into bed?" Her voice pitched.

"Have you lost your mind?" From the sound of her voice, Ashley would come through the phone and strangled her if that were possible. "A man like him doesn't need to play games just to get a woman into bed."

Rubbing the back of her neck, she opened her refrigerator. Cold white walls and a bag of wilted lettuce stared back. "He says he doesn't want to hide what's happening between us."

"You know everyone at work already knows he has a thing for you. It's been the topic of office gossip for months. Speaking of the office, what are you going to do?" Ashley quipped back. Kerrigan almost could see Ashley rolling her neck.

"I hadn't thought that far ahead." Kerrigan jotted down a few items on the pad of paper on the kitchen counter. She'd go shopping later, maybe tomorrow or the next day.

Ashley shrilled loudly through the speaker. "Kerri, ready or not, he's serious about you. I can't believe you didn't sleep with him."

She paced the floor. The thought hit her in the gut like a punch to a punching bag. "That's complicated—has more to do with me than him. I'm just not ready yet." She didn't like the direction of this conversation.

"Sex isn't that complicated. It's not as though you've never done it before…" Ashley's voice suddenly muffled, sounding as if her mouth were cupped. "Oh. My. God," she said in clipped phrases. "Now it all makes sense! You're a virgin, aren't you? Kerri, why didn't you tell me after all these years? Wow, I'm shocked." Ashley screeched loudly through the phone's speaker, the vibration sending the phone tumbling to its side and clattering against the granite.

"I didn't tell you because I'm embarrassed. Besides, you would've only made fun of me."

"That's nothing to be embarrassed about and I wouldn't have made fun of you. Kerri, does he know?" Her tone was serious.

Grabbing the phone from the countertop, she moved from the kitchen into her living room and lay down on her sofa. "Yes, he knows. I was ready and willing, but he wouldn't touch me—doesn't think we're ready. He said he would like to woo me and have me head over heels before we make love. He's very romantic and sentimental that way."

Ashley was stunned into silence for a brief moment. "He said that?" She could hear the excitement in Ashley's voice.

"Yes, he did. Surprised me too."

"I don't know what you did to that man. I think he's in love with you."

Ashley's words gripped her stomach. "He can't be. Sure, we've known each other for a year, but the deeper level of this … whatever this is, I guess relationship, is only weeks old. I don't believe he's in love with me."

"I think he is. Maybe he doesn't even know he's in love, but Axel Christensen is head over heels, in love. Kerri, I think he's your Mr. Right." Kerrigan jerked the phone away from her ear to prevent permanent hearing loss from the shrill of Ashley's voice.

Kerrigan frowned. "What should I do?"

"First, stop panicking. Let yourself fall in love with him too, if you haven't already. Kerri, you've never been in a serious relationship before. Second, take things one step at a time."

"I've never really even dated anyone exclusively, except for Greg, and that was only two months. I know you think I'm weird."

Ashley's voice softened. "No, I don't think you're weird. I actually think that what's happening between you two is beautiful. Just don't panic and take your time. I agree with Axel. He obviously wants things to work with you. Follow your heart."

She loved her friend. Despite the fact that she was outspoken, and at times brash, Ashley understood the boy-girl dynamics better than anyone else did. "Thanks, Ash. I've been so nervous and afraid of screwing this up. You always calm me."

"Hon, I'm excited for you both. You deserve to be happy. I have to go now. With your man being out of town this week, maybe we can do lunch or happy hour."

"Yes, lunch this week would be perfect. I could use some girl time. See you tomorrow."

***

When Kerrigan arrived at work the next day, she immediately called Brenda. "I need your help while Axel is away in New York. I'll come upstairs to give you details." She smiled, hung up the phone and headed to the executive suite. What would Brenda think?

CHAPTER FIFTEEN

Monday, September 24

Axel walked into the hotel room, and a black and white striped gift box on the bed was the first thing he saw. His fingers peeled opened the note attached to the top of the small box.

Axel,

I hope you'll think of me while you're in New York. Here's a little something to keep you safe and warm.

Kerrigan

Placing the note down, he picked up the box and lifted the lid. White tissue paper clung to a plush object stuffed inside. Tearing the paper away, a slow smile spread across his lips, and he let out a hardy laugh. Not pretentious or stuck up, she wasn't like so many of the other women he had encountered. His money and power didn't impress her, and she always considered others ahead of herself. A twinge struck him in the chest. Sitting on the edge of the bed, he pulled out his Blackberry and sent her a message.

10:30 a.m. on Monday, September 24

To: Kerrigan Mulls

From: Axel Christensen

Subject: Hi

Hi Baby,

I landed about an hour ago but just checked into the hotel. I was thinking about you, trying to find a good excuse to email you, but then I opened the box that was left on my bed. My feet and I love the gift you sent. You won't believe this, but I actually forgot to pack socks to lounge around in. My mind has been preoccupied lately, and I'm forgetful these days, so your gift is perfect. I wish I could thank you in person, but I'll be back soon. Are you wearing one of your sexy tight skirts today?

Yours,

A

***

Her pulse raced wildly as she slid the mouse over the new message in her inbox and double-clicked. Her cheeks hurt from smiling so broadly after reading his email. Feeling self-conscious about her uncontrollable grin, she peered over her shoulder, to make sure no one stood in the hall near her doorway. The sound of her fingers tapping the keys echoed in her office.

10:35 a.m. on Monday, September 24

From: Kerrigan Mulls

To: Axel Christensen

Subject: Re: Hi

Hi Axel,

I was thinking about you too. I'm glad you liked the gift. Yes, I'm wearing a skirt today. I didn't know you thought my skirts were sexy. What are you wearing?

Kerrigan

***

11:08 a.m. on Monday, September 24

To: Kerrigan Mulls

From: Axel Christensen
Subject: In the buff
Everything about you is sexy, but I thought you only wore those skirts for my benefit. They've cost me many sleepless nights and lost productivity. I may have to enforce a new dress code policy when I get back – for my eyes only. I just stepped out of the shower. I'm going out to network and grab a bite to eat. Can I call you later tonight?
Yours,
A

***

12:32 p.m. on Monday, September 24
From: Kerrigan Mulls
To: Axel Christensen
Subject: Tease
It's good to know you have such an appreciation for my wardrobe, although I'm truly sorry about the lost productivity. I'll have to use this knowledge to my advantage. Enjoy your networking. I'll talk to you later.
Kerrigan

***

Monday dragged on for her. She was looking forward to Axel's call, but knowing he was unavailable until later that evening, she decided to run errands before going home. She had barely made her way into the apartment, bags tossed haphazardly to the floor and shoes kicked across the room, when the phone rang. Stumbling her way to the table where the handset lay, she answered on the first ring, knowing the call was from Axel. *Get a grip. He's only been gone a few days.* She scolded herself.

Her stomached knotted and twisted in anticipation of his voice. "Hello, Axel?" She hadn't intended to sound so cheerful, longing.

"Yes, it's me. Hi baby." The smile in his voice and his deep low rumble quaked through her body so fiercely that her knees weakened, sinking her to the floor. "How was your day?" He greeted her with equal enthusiasm.

"My day was good, nothing out of the ordinary. I had a good meeting with Rich about two of his accounts. How did your networking go?" Speaking rapidly and winded, she patted her chest and inhaled. A grown woman acting like such a giddy hormonal teenager was ridiculous.

"Slow. There aren't many people here yet. I think most of them are checking in tomorrow morning. That's when the conference officially starts. I should have brought you with me, Kerrigan."

Her pulse raced. "You know I wouldn't have come." The lie flew out of her mouth like an auto response before she could amend the words.

"Oh, baby one day I'm going to make you come," he said, a wicked undercurrent in his tone, followed by a soft chuckle. He was obviously amused with himself for his cunning innuendo.

"Oh? Is that a promise?"

"Sure is. If you keep this up, I'll catch the next flight home and deliver on my promise."

"You wouldn't! We have an agreement, and you have a speech to give." She giggled.

"I would. That agreement can be easily broken. With modern technology, I can give my speech from anywhere, at any time, even after a passionate night of making love to you. Don't tempt me Miss Mulls." She curled her toes, nerve endings firing like guns at a range.

Leaning against the dining room wall, she rubbed her thighs incessantly. "You said we aren't ready yet."

"Hmm, I guess I did say that, didn't I?" he asked coyly.

"Yes, you did."

By this time, she had moved to her bedroom and tossed herself onto the bed. So aroused, she slipped lusty fingers into her panties, touching herself to soothe the ache.

"I don't know what will happen the next time I see you, Kerrigan. All bets are off."

She yanked her hand out of her panties. "Our actions come with consequences," she reprimanded.

"Maybe, but the thought of being with you makes the risk a worthwhile consideration. Besides, I think I can live with the consequences," he said in a serious tone. "Kerrigan, I …"

Before he could finish, she cut him off. His sobering tenor made her shoulders tighten, and her mouth go dry. "I'm open to negotiation when you get back," she said, hoping this was enough to stall him.

"Should I head to the airport now?" he teased.

"Stay in New York. I'll be here when you get back." Nervously, she laughed.

"I'll let you have this one. You're not as sly as you think, sweetheart. This is not over. We'll have this discussion as soon as I get back."

Damn. Busted. At least she had successfully put off the conversation for now.

They talked a while longer about his speech the next day. She admired so many things about him, including his confidence and expertise. She'd seen him present many times, and he was a pro. She knew he'd do a great job, and she had told him so.

Kerrigan let out an exhausted sigh.

"I'll let you go to bed. I just wanted to hear your voice. I need to get some sleep, too. I'm taking my socks off and going to bed. Goodnight baby."

She giggled. "Goodnight, Axel. Good luck with your speech tomorrow."

***

Axel emailed Kerrigan early the next morning.

6:15 a.m. on Tuesday, September 25

To: Kerrigan Mulls

From: Axel Christensen

Subject: Sleepless

Kerrigan,

I wasn't able to sleep much after our conversation, or maybe anxiety about my speech was the cause. I can't call you tonight. I have to attend a banquet this evening, and I'll get in too late. I plan to schmooze like the best of them. There are several prospects I hope to reach out to. I'll talk to you tomorrow.

Yours,

A

***

Later that day, Axel delivered his speech. He talked about what his company was doing to help its most challenged clients achieve substantial wins with innovative and creative strategies.

That evening, he attended the banquet. Several women shamelessly flaunted themselves, hoping to garner his attention.

A woman dressed like a high-priced hooker ready to be worn out in exchange for booze and a few Benjamin's approached him. "Oh my, aren't you Axel Christensen?" Sex and seduction oozed from every pore, the scanty amount of candy apple red spandex she wore as a dress exposed most of them.

"The one and only." He smiled coolly down at the temptress, his eyes widening.

"I'm Mindy." She held out her boney hand, and he dusted her flesh with a light kiss. "You gave an impressive presentation earlier and got me all excited. I could use your direction and expert touch on a little project I have cooking." Long, narrow fingertips painted with bright red polish stroked his forearm, her body language screaming 'fuck me'. "Maybe you and I could go somewhere … for a private session. You can tell me exactly what to do."

Gazing up at him, her pupils dilated and head tilted back, the throbbing vein in her neck, was exposed.

His narrowed eyes raked over her taut body and landed on her hoisted double D implants. Slowly, his tongue ran along his bottom lip. "Hmm," he moaned. Leaning in close, he whispered softly in her ear so that only she was the only recipient of his words. "Miss whatever-your-name-is, I suggest you take an extinguisher to that project you have cooking. Goodnight."

Under normal circumstances, he would have taken her back to his hotel room and given the little vixen exactly what she begged for, but there was nothing normal about his feelings for Kerrigan. Miss Desperation wasn't even temptation.

He turned and walked off, shaking his head, muttering to himself. "I never realized how ugly and unattractive desperation is." The embarrassed and horrified look in her eyes hadn't fazed him one bit. Women threw themselves at Axel all the time, but he had never rejected any of them because of his feelings for someone else. With Kerrigan in the picture, he wanted no one else. He was in deep.

CHAPTER SIXTEEN

Wednesday, September 26

By Wednesday morning, Axel truly missed Kerrigan. He hadn't communicated with her since early the prior morning, and thoughts of her consumed him. Despite what she had said when they last spoke, he knew she would submit willingly to him when the mood was right. He controlled her libido the way a racecar driver controls his vehicle, revving her up and taking her to full throttle in seconds flat.

He wanted to do the right thing, the responsible thing. On several occasions, she had referred to his intentions toward her as noble gestures. There was nothing at all noble about the way his cock throbbed at the sight of her delectable body, smell of her natural scent or thought of her beautiful smile. Even now, in the wee hours of the morning alone in his hotel room, she haunted his senses. Restless, he sat down on his hotel bed with his laptop in hand and banged out an email to her.

5:23 a.m. on Wednesday, September 26
To: Kerrigan Mulls
From: Axel Christensen
Subject: Thinking about you

Hi Baby,

I can't sleep, so I thought I'd email you. My speech went well. This was a good move for our business. The publicity and response have been unbelievable.

I need to talk to you later tonight. Is 10:00 p.m. okay?

Restless in New York,

A

***

9:17 a.m. on Wednesday, September 26

From: Kerrigan Mulls

To: Axel Christensen

Subject: Restless

A,

Congratulations! I'm glad everything is going so well. I had no doubt you'd draw attention and fanfare. You're an excellent speaker, and you have a dynamic personality. Your passion for your company is magnetic. I'm sorry you aren't sleeping well. I'll talk to you tonight at 10:00 p.m.

Kerrigan

Something about his email unnerved her to the core. He had said he needed to talk to her. So inexperienced in romantic dealings and unsure about their relationship, she didn't know if this would be good or bad news. Since his email had been so vague, she contemplated writing back to him to ask if everything were okay, but she decided against it. Inwardly, she braced herself and her heart for the worst.

***

After work, Kerrigan and Ashley went out for drinks. It had been months since the two friends had hung out for happy hour and girl talk. They entered the bar and the heads of five young, hot-blooded males sitting at a table dressed in expensive suites, turned and followed them as they shimmied through the crowded restaurant.

"Do you see the looks we're getting? There's some serious eye candy in here tonight!" Ashley commented.

Kerrigan spotted the table of men who were ogling them. Making eye contact, a handsome sinewy man with sandy colored hair winked. She turned to Ashley. "I'm not in the market. Have at it," she said as they sauntered to their table.

Soon after, they were seated, and the waiter came to take their drink orders.

"My name is Charlie. What can I get you ladies this evening?" he asked.

Ashley ordered first. "Cosmopolitan, please."

"Appletini for me," she said.

With orders in tow, Charlie returned to the bar, leaving them to chat.

"So, how has your week been without lover boy around? I know you miss him."

"I do miss him. We've been emailing or talking every day. He's calling me later tonight …" she said hesitantly, her breath hitching at a pause.

"I sense a 'but'? What is it?" Ashley eyed her speculatively.

She hated when Ashley gave her that look. It usually meant she'd have to spill the beans, and Ashley would clean them up. "But, he said he needs to talk to me tonight. It just feels … ominous."

Ashley rolled her eyes at Kerrigan and smiled. "I don't think you have anything to worry about. I can't imagine Axel going to New York and suddenly deciding that after a year of chasing you that he's done." Ashley regarded her with a gentle smile. "This is the same man who kidnapped you to force you to deal with your feelings. He wouldn't have done that if he weren't serious about you."

She uncrossed her arms, which had been folded over her chest. "I guess you're right. I'm such a nervous wreck."

"Of course I'm right! If there's one thing that I know without a doubt, it's that Axel is crazy about you. He's in love with you. Okay, how much longer are you planning to hold out on him?" Ashley flashed a wicked grin.

She glanced at two nearby tables, satisfied that other patrons weren't paying them any attention, she whispered. "We're in negotiations now." Her cheeks warmed as the words leaped off her tongue. Her foot tapped nervously against the leg of the table.

Her forehead crinkling, Ashley lifted one eyebrow. "Negotiations? You're going to drive that poor man mad. You might as well just give it up. You know you want to."

"Taking the relationship slow was his plan, and now I've rather warmed up to the idea. I think you're right though. The wait is starting to get to him."

"No doubt," Ashley shook her head.

"Waiting is driving me crazy too. Abstinence is probably best though." She still couldn't shake the feeling that he'd end up breaking her heart.

Narrowing her eyes, Ashley stared her down with her girl-you-must-be-nuts look. "Kerri, you're both crazy in love with each other. Yeah, I said 'in love' so don't even debate me on this." Index finger in the air to punctuate her point, Ashley rolled her neck and laid into Kerrigan, reading her Miranda rights. "He's everything you've been waiting for and then some. I'm sorry, but I fail to see how or why abstinence is best."

Ashley, being a supremely confident and independent woman wouldn't understand. Kerrigan couldn't tell her that fear had kept her from fully opening her heart to Axel.

"Perhaps you're right, but this is something that Axel and I have to work through together. He wants to wait, and there's nothing I can do about that."

Ashley's head cocked to one side, her lips pursed. "Like hell there isn't. All you have to do is get that man alone in a room and blink. I'm sure you can get a little more creative than that." Leaning forward over the small table, she grabbed Kerrigan by the wrists. "Show him a little tit and ass, and he won't be able to resist."

Kerrigan kicked the table so hard that it shook. The loud sound drew the attention of several pairs of eyes from patrons at nearby tables landed on them. Her face heated. "I'll take that under advisement," she whispered, and holding her laughter she sunk into her seat. "Ash, do you remember what your first time was like?"

"Wow! That was such a long time ago." Ashley paused, a distant look washed across her face as she reminisced about her first sexual encounter. "Hmm…I remember the pain, but I think it depends on the guy. You know, the feeling depends on his size and how rough or gentle his is. My first time was uneventful—I can't remember much. Hell Kerri, I still can't believe you've never had sex before. By the way, rumor is that Axel carries a pretty big package." Nodding her head, Ashley twisted one corner of her mouth.

Kerrigan squirmed so vigorously in the wooden seat that the chair's legs wobbled and creaked. Her cheeks empurpled as she indulged in the memories of heated exchanges shared between them. "I think I can confirm that rumor."

She thought about their first kiss on his balcony. His erection pressed into her stomach, her knees buckled, and mind went blank. His gray sweat pants dipped low from his waist as he stood in the guest bedroom doorway, walking temptation in the flesh. His bulge protruded so much that she couldn't peel her eyes away, and then when he held her … oh god, the feeling that coursed through her made her head swim.

One moment in particular made her smile burst, remembering their romantic day in the park. She had felt the fullness of Axel's erection pulsing and pressing hard along her inner thigh and against her sex, begging entrance. The hot lead pipe in his pants soldered her tender flesh. She heated at the thought. Fanning her face with her hands, fingers flapping, "That's enough about that. Things are status quo for now," she said as Charlie reappeared with their drinks.

Ashley patted her friend on the arm. "Kerri, I know you're afraid of getting hurt or making a mistake, but I know he loves you. I'm not telling you what to do, but don't let fear rule your heart."

They talked for another hour before leaving. Just outside of the restaurant, they hugged and parted ways. She was appreciative of Ashley's sage advice and insight. Sure, she joked a lot, but she also had words of encouragement.

***

Kerrigan made it home at nine forty-five, just in time for Axel's call. With shaking hands, she flustered as she inserted the key into the lock. The door flung open, and she bolted through. Her handbag landed somewhere between the sofa table and the television stand. Hopping on her left foot, she brought her right foot up and removed her shoe. Then switching feet, she hopped on the right foot and removed her left shoe. She tossed the shoes across the room, and they crashed into the wall.

"Oops! What's wrong with me?" She blurted out loud.

The phone rang. In a fit of fury, she sprinted to the phone and picked it up with anxious Jello fingers.

"Hello." Butterflies fluttered in Kerrigan's stomach.

"Hi baby," he said, his deep soothing baritone drawl stroked her ears.

The moment he spoke, her anxiety melted away. His tone instantly told her that nothing had changed between them.

She sank into her sofa and drew knees up to her chest. "Hi, how was your day? How is the networking going?"

"My day was fine. I met several new people, and I'm even trying to line up a couple of follow-up meetings after the conference ends. I don't want to talk about work. Kerrigan … I" he paused, as though he was considering the words he wanted to say. "I miss you."

"I miss you too, Axel," she said.

"Do you know what I'm doing right now?" he asked. "I'm staring out the window at New York City, and thinking of you. I can't get you off my mind. I've also been thinking seriously about our arrangement and moving things forward. It's a giant step, but I'm ready. Are you ready?"

"Can we talk about this when you get back?" Her voice strained to remain calm.

"Okay. We can talk later, but I'm giving you fair warning now. That agreement won't last much longer, especially since you can't keep your hands off me," he laughed.

"What am I going to do with you?" She shook her head.

"I have some ideas. I'll show you as soon as I get back home." His low, seductive tone made her heart hammer in her chest.

"I'm beginning to think that's all you want from me," she said in a joking tone.

"Kerrigan, I'm not going to lie. I do want you badly, but I want all of you—body, heart, mind and soul. Not seeing you in days is driving me crazy. I can't touch you or be near you. I really miss you. I need…" His voice, his words, his intonation was sultry and smooth.

Pressing her chin into her knees, she relished his words before the doubt took residence in her brain.

She cut him off again. "Here, I'm texting something to you to get you through the next few days. Consider it your inspiration until you get back."

Axel retrieved the message and then clicked on the photo to enlarge it. "Holy shit! Kerrigan, are you trying to give me a heart attack or just send me straight to bedlam?" The picture of her in the barely-there bikini on the beach where she and Ashley had gone that past summer was a favorite.

"Do you like it?"

"I love it. God, you're beautiful. You realize this makes it even harder for me to honor that damned agreement." She was certain erotic thoughts of what he wanted to do to her were running through his head. The same thoughts ran through Kerrigan's mind.

"Glad you like it. I hate to go, but I'm tired. You need to try to sleep too, Mr. Restless. Did you want to talk about anything else before I go?" She hoped he wasn't going to start pouring out his heart again. That terrified her.

"I did want to talk about something else, but that can wait. I won't be getting any sleep anytime soon. Your photo has my pulse racing now. I think you can imagine what the male part of my anatomy is doing too. I'm going to work out, and then come back for a cold shower."

***

Axel changed his clothes and headed down to the hotel's gym. At every opportunity, he glanced at Kerrigan's photo stored on his cell phone. A gangly brunette woman who could benefit from a burger and fries instead of a workout was the only other person in the gym. Desperation masked behind beady eyes traced his steps the instant he entered the room. Axel jammed headphones into his ears signaling his disinterest.

Before Kerrigan, he might have found the woman attractive and may have even engaged her in conversation to find out more about her, but no other woman could hold a light to Kerrigan's brilliance. The brown-haired woman in the gym was dulled and tedious compared to her.

"Hi. I see I'm not the only person in this hotel who loves a late-night workout. It's good to have the company." She smiled, bobbing up and down on the elliptical trainer.

He frowned, and then removed an ear bud. "Don't waste your time or mine, sweetheart. I'm here to workout, not chat." He turned his head away, replaced his earpiece and tuned her out, continuing his regimen.

***

Axel leaned against the counter thrumming his restless fingers on the slick surface. A short round man with a receding hairline stood on the other side, his ear pressed against the handset. After several minutes, he thanked the person on the other end of the call and hung up, placing the handset into the cradle that was mounted to the faux brick wall.

The stubbly man turned to meet Axel's eyes. "Are you the young man who called about the Atlanta order?" He lifted calloused fingers to remove the pencil resting behind his ear.

A grin spread across Axel's face. "Yes. May I see them? I'm very particular. They have to be perfect." He retrieved his wallet from the rear pocket of his black slacks. "Are you certain your Atlanta shop has the same quality?"

"Yes sir, I'm positive." The man smiled and then scribbled on a yellow sticky note. "What's the delivery day?"

"Sunday."

"Our shop in Atlanta is closed on Sundays. How's Monday?"

"Monday won't work. I need Sunday delivery, and I'm prepared to make it worth your effort." Axel smiled and handed over his credit card. "Can you make this happen?"

His bowling ball head seemed to glow. "I believe Sunday will work just fine."

CHAPTER SEVENTEEN

Sunday, September 30

Warm water cascaded over Kerrigan's shoulders like liquid sunshine. Showering in her bathroom was comforting. She thought about the many conversations she had shared with Axel, how he looked at her and how he touched her. Could Ashley be right, about Axel's feelings? Had he fallen in love with her? The thought of being in love was too much, too soon.

Raindrops beat heavily against the sliding glass doors. A towel wrapped around her damp skin, Kerrigan made her way to the balcony and slid open the doors to let the sound of the torrential downpour permeate her bedroom. Delivered earlier in that day the fresh bouquet of roses sat on her dresser, and added a sensual aroma. Eloquent words brought tears to Kerrigan's eyes each time she read the note.

To a beautiful woman with a beautiful soul,

I can't wait to see you, to feel the warmth of your skin against mine, to taste your sweet lips. Your beauty leaves me speechless and wanting. Your tender heart gives me peace. Your gentle smile lifts my spirit. I want you to know how you make me feel. I want you in every way imaginable—body, heart, mind and soul. I never thought I had it in me to say these words to anyone, but you inspire me the way no other woman ever could. Because of you, I'm a rescued man.

Rescued in New York

Kerrigan organized herself for the next day and climbed into bed, enjoying the sounds of the falling rain. The time was nearly eleven o'clock, and she hadn't heard from Axel all day, not even a text message.

He was traveling, but to let silence go between them for an entire day was unlike him. A little worried, she leaned her head back against her headboard. Twitchy fingers clambered across the nightstand, searching. Catching up on the latest celebrity gossip would calm her nerves and help her sleep. Just as she retrieved the magazine, the phone rang. Jolted, she glanced at the caller ID, an unknown caller. A knot formed in her throat. The phone rang again. Who could be calling so late? She tossed the magazine down next to her on the bed, leaned over and picked up the phone.

"Hello."

"Hi," the husky voice said back.

"Axel?" she asked.

"The one and only. Were you expecting someone else to call you so late?"

"No, I wasn't expecting anyone to call me, not even you," she said, a tingling sensation started in her toes and moved through her body in waves. "Where are you? Are you home?"

He cleared his throat. "I'm close. I know we spoke a day ago, but I miss your voice. I can't wait to see you again."

"I miss you too." She smiled into the handset.

"What are we going to do about that?" His voice sent a shiver up her spine.

"What do you mean? Won't I see you tomorrow?" she asked.

At that precise moment, there was a loud knock at the front door. Startled, she gasped loudly.

"What was that?" he asked.

"I think there's someone knocking on my door. Can you hold on a minute?"

"Are you expecting someone at this hour?" The displeasure in his tone wasn't hard to miss.

"No, but I need to at least check out the sound."

"Kerrigan, I don't like that you live alone. Take the phone with you. You never know who could be out there. Are you dressed?" His tone was brusque.

"Okay, I'm taking the phone with me, and yes, I have on my robe."

"What are you wearing underneath?"

"I'm wearing a red nightie, but now is not the time for phone sex."

"That's not why I asked. Just make sure you tie your robe around you properly."

She headed into the dimly lit living room, delicate light bounced off the walls and ceiling, casted a surreal glow. As she neared the door, another loud banging noise came from the other side. Her heart pounded hard. She peeked through the peephole but couldn't see anyone.

"Hello, who's out there?" She demanded.

"Open the door, Kerrigan," the familiar voice boomed.

She looked through the peephole again. "I won't open the door until I know who's out there."

Her heart stopped, and her stomach clenched. She plastered herself against the door to keep upright. Axel stood there with a concupiscent grin anchored to his face. He held up his cell phone for her to see.

With jittery hands, she disconnected the phone call, fumbled with locks and the knob until the door opened. "What are you doing here? You just got back." Her glaze swept over him, and she became dizzy. Anxiety still heightened, she held onto the doorframe for strength. "Do you know what time it is? Aren't you exhausted?" She rattled off, her eyes wide, and legs trembled.

He leaned against the doorframe, his hand covering hers. "I had to see you, so I came here directly from the airport." His chest heaved as though he had run the whole way from New York. "Don't worry about work tomorrow. Your boss won't mind if you play hooky or come in late." His greedy eyes swept over her.

She feasted on his body. He was soaking wet, having been drenched from the storm, and damn if that didn't make him that much sexier. "And why would I play hooky or come in late tomorrow?"

"If you let me in, you'll find out. Do you want me to stand outside all night soaking wet?" He pushed against the grains of the solid wood door, opened it wide and walked through.

Kerrigan moved aside, clearing a path for him. He pivoted, and then closed and locked the door. Taking measured steps, he turned around slowly and stepped closer to her. His strong hands moved to her waist and he pulled her close, drawing her flush against his hard drenched body. She wrapped her arms around his neck. They locked eyes, her temperature rose, and her palms dampened as the inferno within her ignited almost instantly. She was captivated by the magnitude of his emotion for her. The look in his eyes indicated the trance he was under, mesmerized by her. Every nerve in her body screamed.

He leaned down slowly, crushing his lips against hers; he kissed her deeply and passionately as if drawing on her breath for life, and then he released a deep guttural groan. The room was spinning around her, and her knees buckled. He pulled her closer, tightening his grip on her and keeping her upright. His erection pressed firmly against her stomach, her hard nipples pierced his chest. A rush of warm moisture readied between her thighs and she ached, her sex clenching. Her fingers dug through the fine hairs at the nape of his neck, drawing him into her kiss. Pulling away abruptly, he distanced himself from her, taking a few steps back.

"I missed you baby," he said huskily as his eyes examined her soft hair flowing gracefully down her back. A ravenous gaze glided to her perky breast thrust forward, slid down golden muscular legs pouring from the bottom of her thigh-length silk robe, and then landed on her perfectly manicure toes polished in pastel pink. "Touching you baby, does feel so good."

Lost, she gazed into his blue eyes. "I missed you too. Thank you for the beautiful flowers and the note. I loved them." Winded from their sensual kiss, she found catching her breath difficult.

"I'm glad you liked them. I meant every word." A crooked smile traveled across his lips, and he closed the distance between them again.

She placed her hands on his chest. "Don't most people pick up the phone and call before showing up at someone's house at this hour?" She teased, her voice almost a whisper.

He placed his hand under her chin and lifted her face, his eyes meeting hers, holding her tightly against his torso. "I did call," he said, and then grinned, his eyes dark, drawn to a sliver covered by heavy lids.

"I thought we were going to see each other at work tomorrow?"

"I wanted to see you as soon as I got back into town. It's been a long week. I couldn't wait, Kerrigan."

"What's going to happen at work when you miss me? You can't linger in my doorway all day long. Are you planning to move me into your office with you?" She teased.

"Don't tempt me. The thought did cross my mind."

"You're crazy." She giggled.

"Crazy for you."

Thunder roared loudly overhead, and the lights flickered. Startled, she jolted.

"Come on. Let's go to bed," he said, flashing a dangerous smile at her.

"What?" she asked, her voice raising a few octaves as she backed away from him.

He advanced at her retreat, stepping closer and closer as she moved away until she felt the smooth cool wall against her back. He was always pinning her between a wall and his hard body.

"You seem to find yourself in this position with me quite often," he teased.

"You seem to like putting me in this position." Playfully, she shoved him and pressed her small hands against his bulging biceps, not budging him even an inch.

"I like you in any position where I can be close to you."

The butterflies in her belly danced wildly now, and she panted, winded. Her knees were doing that wobbly thing again, and she steadied herself by clinging to his arms. He leaned down and gently whispered in her ear. "I don't know what kind of guy you think I am, but there will be no funny business young lady. I'll sleep on my side of the bed, and you'll sleep on yours."

"Axel, I have a small queen-sized bed," she said breathlessly.

"Then I guess we have to bunk. I call tops."

"You're nuts! No bunking. You stick to your side of the bed … Wait! What am I saying? You can't sleep in my bed, Axel!"

She pushed against him with more force this time, but there was no use. He couldn't be moved.

He grabbed her wrists and pinned them against the wall at her side. "Come on. The hour is late." She almost saw the savage energy that pulsed through his body.

Her mouth went dry, adrenaline coursed through her veins and her insides vibrated. She knew where this was heading, but before she could protest further, he released her wrists and grabbed her by one hand. "I assume your bedroom is this way," he muttered as he pulled her down the hallway.

She swallowed hard. "Fine, but I'm serious. No funny business."

He released her hand once they reached the bedroom. Shuffling across the room to the other side of the bed, she turned to walk to her closet, but a loud clank caught her attention, and she spun around.

"What are you doing?" Her voice trembled.

She watched him loosen and pull a black belt through the loops of his pants. "I'm getting ready for bed. I don't sleep in jeans. I normally sleep in my boxers, unless you'd be more comfortable if I slept in the buff." He tossed the belt onto a bedside chair.

"No! Keep your underpants on. I think you should also wear your t-shirt," she said, realizing she was practically yelling.

"This is a small bed. I'll be too hot in this t-shirt with your body heat so close to me. Besides, my shirt is soaking wet. Either the shirt goes, or the boxers go. Which is it?" He flashed a sinister grin, and she warmed, heat rushed to her face.

Winged feet carried Kerrigan to the bedroom closet, and she retrieved a towel. "Fine, keep the underwear on."

"That's a wise choice. I wouldn't want you to get out of hand tonight." His electrifying grin sent a bolt through her body and her insides quivered.

She couldn't believe that he was there, ready to sleep in her bed. Denim slid down his muscular tanned thighs as he lifted one foot at a time, and then stepped out of his jeans, tossing them onto the chair. She handed him the towel and watched as he dabbed the beads of moisture away. He stood there for a moment shirtless in his boxers with a cock hard as steel and every muscle in his glistening chest rippling, and then he climbed into bed. Biting at her nails and curling her toes around the loops of the plush tan carpet, warm moisture surged between her thighs. Why did the man have to be so damn hot?

She removed her robe, exposed one brown shoulder, and then the other as he watched, staring a hole through her revealing nightie. His eyes fixed to her swollen bosom, firm nipples erect as they poked against the red fabric. She hoped her breasts wouldn't spill out. Her lingerie was barely long enough to cover her behind. His eyes slithered down her thighs and legs, giving her heart palpitations.

He had admitted to always feeling horny around her, but being in her bed and watching her undress must have been the reason his cock was at full attention, saluting her proudly and tenting the blanket. He licked his lips as she scrambled in next to him. Her small bed put them closer than she had expected. She lay down as close to the edge as possible and folded her arms across her belly, not sure what else to do with herself. The lamp on her nightstand was on. With abrupt motion, he leaned across, almost lying fully on top of her and turned off the light.

She gasped.

"Can't get much sleep with the light on, now can we?" he asked, the deep rumble of his voice stroking her ears.

She shuddered inside as his muscular body grazed hers, the ridge of his hard cock pushing sharply into her thigh. His impetuous action heightened her libido, her sex swollen and aching, a sudden desire to be filled with him.

The only light in the room now came from the occasional flash of lighting and the twinkling lights of the city below, dimly illuminating the darkness through the sheer cream-colored curtains that covered the large glass doors that led to the balcony. Rain had begun to fall harder outside. The stillness of the room echoed loudly, their harsh breathing and erratic heart beats the only sounds competing against the storms raging outside and within them both. She was careful not to touch him or else she might stir the raging beast within him, one that she wouldn't be able to tame and wouldn't want to stop.

***

His restlessness was motivated by a different drive altogether, his desire to claim Kerrigan's heart and satisfy his sexual thirst. He was pure, raw masculine heat. He needed her, wanted her and planned to have her, tonight. Neither of them would get much sleep.

He glanced over at her. She was staring up at the ceiling, too. He knew why he was there and she was about to find out.

"Kerrigan," his voice was low and thick, breaking the uneasiness of the night.

"Yes," she replied, in a nearly inaudible whisper.

"You know why I'm here. You know what I want."

"What do you mean?" Her voice cracked.

"You know exactly what I mean. It's what we both want only you're afraid to admit it. It's time to take our relationship to the next level."

"Axel, you said we needed to take things slowly. You said neither of us is ready. I thought we were going to talk about the agreement," she protested, and he could hear the anxiety building in her.

"Forget what I said. There's no need for discussion. I'm about to break that damn agreement in the worse way. We're both ready, and tonight, you belong to me baby."

"You said you wanted to respect me, to woo me."

He shifted, and repositioned himself on his side with his elbow on the bed and his head propped up by his large hand. Leaning over, he looked down at her sweetly, peering into her longing gaze. She was so beautiful lying there beneath him. He stroked her cheek gently with his free hand and she leaned into his touch, trembling and eyes wide.

"I have nothing but respect for you. The fact that I'm lying here in your bed means I'm doing a good job wooing you so far, wouldn't you say? Let me give you what you're too afraid to admit you want—what we both want."

"Axel, I'm afraid if we do this, you'll get what you want, and I'll end up getting hurt."

"Kerrigan, I don't just want sex. I don't want to hurt you. Tonight is only the beginning."

He had fallen for her. Saying the words aloud to her would feel right, but he held back.

She swallowed hard. Nothing, she said or did would prevent the inevitable. Her affection ran just as deeply as his did. After all, he was sure Kerrigan knew that letting him into her home at that late hour would only lead to one thing—he would make love to her for the first time that night.

CHAPTER EIGHTEEN

There had been no doubt in Axel's mind what would happen the minute his plane landed. Neither distance nor time would get in the way of his mission. Tonight, he would cherish every inch of her body until she begged him to stop, the way he had done it at least a hundred times in his imagination.

He couldn't remember the exact moment it happened, but somewhere along the way, the lust had morphed into something else. Tonight, he would lay claim to her heart and shatter her insecurities.

***

Axel leaned down, caressed her face gently with his hand and devoured her lips with his passionate kiss.

He peeled himself away. "Baby, just tell me if you want me to stop. I'll be slow and gentle, but you have to tell me if I hurt you or if you want me to stop, okay?"

"Oh … Okay." Her voice shook. Barely able to speak, her nerves rendered her speechless. He resumed his sensual assault on her mouth, kissing and licking her lips, and tasting her sweet honey as she trembled underneath him, barely able to return his kisses.

"Relax, baby. I know you're scared. I won't do anything to you that I know you can't handle. You trust me?"

Staring into his heated gaze, her eyes widened. "I think so."

Leaning down, he kissed her forehead. "That's not good enough. Kerrigan, I want you to trust me. I'm not here to break your heart. Do you trust me?" He leaned into the crook of her neck—his eyes closed inhaling her natural scent.

"Yes, I trust you." Her hushed tone muttered softly into his ear.

"Are you on birth control?" he asked.

"Yes."

Lifting his head from her haven, he stroked her quivering bottom lip with the pad of his thumb. "Do you want me to use a condom?" Gazing into her eyes, "I don't want to use one with you. You okay with that?" His tone was tender.

Her heart pounded hard in her chest against his. "I think so."

He hadn't been with another woman in at least ten months, and he had always used condoms every time in the past. Until now, he'd never really thought about not using one.

"I want to feel you, and I want you to feel me, skin on skin, but I want you to be sure, Kerrigan. I'll use one if you want me to." Her eyes darted, avoiding his gaze. "Kerrigan, look at me."

Peering up at him, she blinked rapidly. "No, you don't have to use a condom. I trust you." Her gaze was unsteady, and her tone wavered.

"Are you sure? I want you to be absolutely sure."

She swallowed hard. "Yes, I'm sure." Kerrigan closed her eyes and turned away. She couldn't believe what she was about to do, with Axel Christensen no less. He had given her fair warning, and she wanted this to happen. Hell, she had practically willed him to show up.

He slid masculine hands down the front of a sheer nightie, fingers dancing across Kerrigan's stomach and to the bottom of the short garment. His hand moved smoothly underneath as he slowly massaged every inch of her bare supple skin, fingers sliding across her stomach and working their way up to her heavenly mounds.

Eager fingers found her breasts, kneading and cupping one in his large masculine hand. His index finger and thumb pulled and rolled her hard nipple until she released a small yelp. Slipping his hand from underneath her gown, he motioned for her to sit up. His fingers inched to the strap of her nightie. He yanked down one strap and then the other until they both were free from her arms.

Riveted to the sight of her naked caramel breasts, "So beautiful," his voice was hoarse and raspy. "I want to savor every part of you." Hot lips pressed into the small of her neck, searing Kerrigan's tender flesh. "Baby, lie down and raise your hips. I want you out of this nightie."

A scintillating stare fastened her eyes to his. Her lean hips hoisted high, he yanked the garment from her body and tossed the silken threads to the side. She looked beautiful lying there only wearing a black lace thong, her breasts exposed.

He turned his attention back to her perky peaks. His mouth descended on one, licking and sucking tender flesh sweet and succulent like ripened fruit as she writhed and moaned. Her back arched, thrusting her breasts upwards as he continued feasting on her delectable bosom. He loved how she felt with her arms wrapped around his shoulders, as though she needed him for support. He loved that she clung to him for strength, wanted what he offered and trusted him with her heart.

His hand busily caressed her thighs and made its way to the soaking wet heat between her legs. He gently spread her thighs apart. Finally reaching his destination, he dipped his hand into the top of her panties until his fingers found the folds of her soft, warm sex, gently stroking her until she whimpered.

To Axel, her sheer lace panties were a nuisance. Tussling with the thongs as he tugged them down her legs and tossed them over his shoulder, they sailed across the room and landed on the floor. Knowing her innocence, he decided not to dip his fingers into her; he would save her virgin sweetness for their full sexual union, when his cock would surge into her depths.

The rain fell harder now and all around them thunder boomed loudly. Wet beads of raindrops splashed against the glass panes. Strong gusts of wind blew in through the doors, which were slightly cracked open, and the sheer curtains danced wildly about.

***

He positioned himself in front of her. Bending her knees and spreading her legs widely apart to accept his girth, he stared at her sex.

"Open your eyes baby. You're beautiful and delightfully soft. I want to see you, and I want you to see me," he said affectionately.

He knelt forward and kissed the slick wetness of her sex, first with his lips and then inserting his tongue between her petals, he French-kissed her delicate flower. Her body quivered all over as he continued his oral stimulation. Her nectar flowed sweetly for him, and he lapped greedily at her essence. She tasted so damn good, like sweet licorice. The way she moaned, he knew the sensation had overwhelmed her, but he wouldn't let her climax like this. He wanted her to savor the joy of complete rapture when he was buried nine inches deep inside her for the first time while she screamed his name.

He came up to meet her lips with a kiss. "Damn, you're sweet. Taste how sweet you are."

He lifted himself up so that they were face-to-face. Time to get down to business. Dipping his head, he kissed her softly, continuing the invasion of her mouth with his tongue as he lay between her legs. She lay there ready for him.

***

She could feel the length of his erection piercing her thigh through his boxers. Although she had never felt a naked penis before, she had seen them in movies and magazines, and his large size scared her. He raised himself up, and then stood beside the bed, the massive protruding bulge strained to break free.

His hand moved to the band on his boxer briefs, slowly snatching them down. Finally freed, his stiff rod sprung out. Stretching her eyes wide, she gasped. She couldn't believe how large he was. She hoped her shock wasn't visible. Stealing another glance, her bulging eyes darted away, embarrassed for having watched him. The thought of what they were about to do flooded her heart with anxiety. This now seemed like a bad idea.

"Look at me, Kerrigan. You don't have to be embarrassed to look at me," he said.

"I don't think I can't do this. You're too big to fit inside me," her voice trembled.

"Baby, I know you're afraid. I'll be gentle. I'll go very slowly. I'll fit inside you. You trust me, right?" His tone was low and soothing.

"Yes." Her shaky tone bordered on the edge of panic.

He leaned down and kissed her tenderly, his hands moving slowly over her breasts, down her stomach and between her thighs again. Warm desire built at her core, soaking her between the thighs and drenching his fingers as he vigorously worked her clitoris. Her back arched up, taken by the pleasure of his touch.

Kneeling between her legs, he spread them apart with his hands and surged forward, the tip of his cock pausing at her moist entrance. He saw the fear in her eyes, and her trembling hands clung to his shoulders.

He kissed her deeply, and then looked into her eyes. "Kerrigan, I know you're afraid, but I want you to understand that what's happening between us is more than sex. I want you, body, heart, mind and soul. I need you. Only you."

***

She could feel the tears building. What she felt for him was too strong, and she realized that she couldn't stop herself now, even if she tried. She wanted to believe his beautiful words, but in a state of confusion and scared, everything overwhelmed her. What was wrong with her?

"I'm afraid. Everything is happening so fast. Everything is changing," she blurted out.

"I know baby. Everything is changing, but don't be afraid of this or me. Let me make love to you tonight. Let me show you how much I care for you. Do you want me?" His voice, low and husky, and pleading.

"Yes, I want you, Axel," she whispered breathlessly, knowing that at least she wasn't confused about her sexual desire. She wanted him so badly that her core ached for him and her sex clenched.

His body rocked back and forth, the tip of his hard shaft pressed between her petals, tapping her opening. She braced herself for the impact of his massive cock invading her. He slowly eased into her and then pulled out. She gasped. He did it again, this time pressing deeper until most of his cock went inside her. She gasped louder this time, pain taking over.

He eased in and out of her until all of him was inside. His face went blurry and she closed her eyes, fighting the tears back. The physical pain alone hadn't brought on, the sudden urge to cry. It was her conflicting emotions, ecstasy, pain, pleasure, fear and hope. In his hands, her heart crumbled.

***

He knew it would take patience tonight. He entered her slowly, breaking through her virginity and stretching her walls to accommodate his size. She whimpered softly and then suddenly cried out in pain. Tears that he thought he had seen in her eyes now spilled onto her cheeks. His size must have been too much for her to handle.

He stilled his movements and stroked her cheek. "Sweetheart, you're trembling and crying. I'm not hurting you, am I? Do you want me to stop?"

"No, don't stop," she replied in a raspy whisper.

He frowned. "Are you sure? I don't want to hurt you. That's the last thing I ever want to do."

***

The tenderness of his voice and words stroked her heart. His touch felt so good that it alone was worth the risk. Maybe Ashley was right—she needed to stop thinking and just feel. Tonight, she wanted him, and he wanted her. Tomorrow would bring whatever it would bring.

"I'm sure. I want you, Axel."

He smiled, dusted her lips lightly with his kiss, and then gazed down into her eyes while gently wiping away her tears with his thumbs. "Kerrigan, if you had any doubts before tonight, I want you to understand that you belong to me. Your body and heart belong to me now, and I surrender myself to you."

He moved inside her again, thrusting with such force that her eyes rolled to the back of her head, and an uncontrollable gasp for breath escaped her lungs, the feeling both amazing and overpowering. She would analyze his words tomorrow. Tonight, she would allay her fears and submit to him.

***

He surged deeper and deeper into her, inch by antagonizing inch until she received all nine inches of him. She was so tight that entering her had been slightly painful for him. With each inch, he hammered into her harder. Her body writhed and trembled with frantic jerks. He tempered her movements with the weight of his large body on top of her small frame. She moaned and whimpered softly. He loved the sweet, seductive sounds she made.

With his lips crushed over hers, he captured her soft cries. He knew taking Kerrigan would be emotional for them both. He also knew she would have to endure the pain of his manhood invading her for the first time. She didn't motion for him to stop and he was careful to be gentle with her.

Being inside her felt so good and he continued his slow rhythmic pounding, grinding deeper and increasing his tempo, he slammed into her harder and faster, stretching her with each blow. Her breathing was erratic, but she wasn't crying anymore. With each powerful thrust he gave, she panted more heavily and wildly. She loosened her grip on him, and her hands fell to either side of her head. He captured her hands, his fingers entwined in hers. They were at last one in the flesh.

***

Kerrigan could feel every inch of his throbbing cock inside her. She felt him in the pit of her stomach. The pain and pleasure were simultaneous and intense as he consumed her. His thrusts became harder as he pressed deeper into her. She loved the feeling of him claiming her, him burrowing himself deep inside her. The sensation was sweet torture and ecstasy all at once. Gasping for air, she broke free of his lips and turned her head.

Her moans were soft, sensual and erotic. "Ah. Ah. Hmm. Ah." He filled her completely.

"You okay baby?" he asked hoarsely.

"Hmm..." She didn't speak with words as he continued pounding hard into her, only returning incoherent pants, under the heavy fog of sexual sedation.

"Feels good?" he questioned her again.

"Yes, you feel so good," she rasped.

***

That was his cue. Her pain was gone, replaced by pleasure. He would fuck her deep and hard all night long until she could take no more. He wanted her to feel his passion, his desire, his longing for her. He pulled out most of himself and slammed into her hard. Soft seductive moans escaped her.

With parted lips, brows pressed together and the cling of her legs wrapped around him, her response was pure unfiltered pleasure. Repeating this motion, he continued plowing into her, unrestrained and reaching her depths. With each powerful thrust, she jolted and trembled hard. He raised himself up and lifted both of her legs onto his shoulders allowing him deeper penetration. He crashed hard into her, and the wave of pleasure so intense that she screamed his name over, and over again.

Her legs shook with tremors, and she bordered the edge of ecstasy, her head spinning and sex clenching, nearing the ultimate release. With her hands no longer bound by his, she clung to his shoulders as though her life depended on it. She gripped him so tight that he could feel her nails pressing into his skin, her fingers tightening and loosening in sync with his powerful thrusts.

***

Relentless, Axel showed no mercy on her as her sex wrapped tightly around his cock. He gave her all of himself, hard, rough and wild, slamming into her so deep that he consumed her, and she was all sensation, she was his. She took him in equal measure, raising her hips to accept his powerful thrusts. She never imagined sex would feel that good. The walls of her sex clamped tightly around his hard shaft, and suddenly she felt as if she had burst into a million points of light, the feeling overpowering her with its stark intensity.

Needing a release, she screamed his name repeatedly as every nerve ending in her body fired at once, and she trembled uncontrollably. Slowly the feeling subsided into calm. Dizzy, but elated, she now had an appreciation for the expressions 'mind-blowing' and 'toe-curling' sex and they were understatements.

***

Axel lay in awe. Kerrigan radiated light as she climaxed for him. He groaned loudly. Not letting go earlier had been hard for him. He had been determined to bring her pass the pain of virginity to the apex of pleasure before he would allow himself to explode. As soon as she found her release, he followed. Grinding deeply and firmly into her, he stilled and released his load deep inside her, coating every inch of her walls with his seed. He had never had an encounter like this, the experience had been so much more than sex.

Axel remained motionless, still firmly erect and inside her. He loved the feeling of her warmth stretched around him. Her body went limp, weary with exhaustion.

He scanned her eyes, caressing her cheek tenderly. "Kerrigan, did I hurt you? Are you all right?"

"Yes, I'm okay." Her words were spoken softly, breathy.

He studied her beautiful face, flustered and bright-eyed. "How do you feel?" he asked, tenderly stroking her cheek.

She placed her small hand on his chest. "The blinders have come off as if I'm seeing for the first time. How about you?"

He chuckled softly at her thoughtfulness. He wanted her first time to be perfect and yet after giving her virginity to him, she was concerned about him. He leaned down, kissed her tenderly on the forehead and then pulled away. "You're an amazing woman. I feel the same way as you do, blinders off."

He knew his heart had found a home. "Get some rest, sweetheart. I'm not done with you yet," he warned, pulling her close and wrapping his body around her protectively.

They drifted off into a light sleep.

***

He had ravished her unreservedly, making passionate love to her all throughout the night. Hours had passed. It was after five o'clock in the morning after their last bout. He gently lowered her legs from over his shoulders.

"Sweetheart, you okay? How do you feel? Did I hurt you?"

Her eyes were heavy, but she managed to speak a few words. "I'm tired and sore, but I'm fine." She had never known such delicious pain and pleasure all at once. Axel had shattered her senses and blown her mind, and she knew her heart was in serious jeopardy.

She gasped and winced as he pulled out of her slowly. He wrapped her in his arms again, her head nestled against his chest, and her hair cascaded onto his abdomen. With his arms and legs enveloping her, he nuzzled her soft hair.

Months of chasing Kerrigan had finally paid off. She nestled in the safety of his arms. His heart pounded in his chest and he breathed deeply, his insides cleared of anxiety. Sex with a woman wasn't novel, but he had never made love to a woman before tonight. Suddenly, the realization dawned on him. He needed to tell her what was in his heart, and coming to terms with the decision hadn't been difficult for him.

"I love you baby. I want your heart, and I'm ready to give you mine. I want you for the rest of my life, and I want to be the man you need," he whispered sweetly into her ear as he held her close.

She must have been too exhausted to comprehend his words because there was no reply. He glanced down at her beautiful face and discovered that she had slipped away into a deep slumber. A nagging thought formed in his head and his gut churned. His eyes fixed on her. There was a hidden emotion captive behind her eyes whenever she looked at him—fear. He wondered if her eyes would look differently tomorrow. Heavily laden with random thoughts, his mind cleared. Soon after, his heavy eyelids shut, and he drifted off to sleep.

The story continues in book two, Closer To You.

Excerpt from Closer To You

***

The morning came crashing into Kerrigan's senses and her eyes fluttered open. Had last night been a dream? The thought was fleeting as soon as she registered the pain between her legs and deep in her belly. Axel had left her there alone. A million thoughts raced through her mind all at once. The most terrifying of them, he had taken her virginity, and now he would discard her. She tried to move, but every limb ached. Rolling over, she reached for the clock on her nightstand. Ten o'clock. *Shit!* Her manager Marie would be livid.

Then she spotted the small folded piece of paper next to the clock. Nausea came over her as her fingers clumsily opened the note. She released the breath she hadn't realized she held as she began to read.

About Lauren H. Kelley

Lauren began writing short stories in high school, but abandoned her first love to pursue a business degree and career in corporate America. A late bloomer to her true calling and craft, she finally figured out what she wanted to do with her life--write! Growing up in a multicultural family, she was exposed to diversity from an early age. She has always had an appreciation and respect for multicultural romance and aims to bridge the racial divide through her novels and short stories. She currently resides in the Southeast.

Buy Closer To You

Visit laurenhkelley.com for the next titles
in the Suits in Pursuit series.

Closer To You (book two)
Take Me Down (coming in 2014)

Find Lauren H. Kelley:
laurenhkelley.com
Facebook.com/authorlaurenhkelley
Twitter: @laurenhkelley

CPSIA information can be obtained at www.ICGtesting.com
Printed in the USA
LVOW12s2218110515

438055LV00025B/647/P

9 780989 871426